The Girl
on
Gander
Green Lane

by
M J Hardy

Contents

Note from The Author

A word of warning. There is a strong theme of domestic violence that runs through this book.

This abuse is unacceptable and victims should seek help immediately. If you can relate to any of this tell your family, a friend or a trained professional. You do not have to suffer and if anything, I hope this book illustrates that fact.

All of the quotes used at the beginning of every chapter were obtained from:

https://www.brainyquote.com

PROLOGUE

"You only get one life and it's up to you how you shape it. Like an empty patch of ground, you can take it and mould it into something magnificent, breath-taking and beautiful. It takes courage and determination but if you believe enough it will be the greatest reward.

There is no room for complacency. No allowances and no second chances. Your dream will become your reality if you know how to make it happen.

Crush your opponents and stand tall among men. Never waiver for a second because that will be your downfall. Nurture, protect and don't be afraid to fight for what you believe in. Take no prisoners and show no mercy because once you show weakness, you will fail.

Never lose control of your own life because that's where the problems begin. Like an unwanted virus they seep into the cracks of an otherwise perfect life and taint and destroy the beauty you have created. Do not let the control slip from your fingers because once it's gone, it will never return. You are the only one who can make your life count for something beautiful and meaningful and it's up to you to make that happen.

Do you understand me, son?"

"Yes mummy."

"Will you live by my words and become the man I know you can be?"

"Yes mummy."

"Have you learned your lesson?"

"Yes mummy."

"Then what do you have to say to me?"

"I'm sorry mummy."

"And?"

"I love you mummy."

CHAPTER ONE

'Today I choose life. Every morning when I wake up, I can choose joy, happiness, negativity, pain... To feel the freedom that comes from being able to continue to make mistakes and choices - today I choose to feel life, not to deny my humanity but embrace it.' - Kevyn Aucoin

There is that moment of the day where the world stills as if waiting for something to happen that will put me out of my misery. Maybe today will be that day. In a way, I wish it was. I need it to happen because living with the inevitability is worse than the certainty it will happen.

I go about my daily routine wondering if this will be my last. As I straighten the towel in the family bathroom, I do so on autopilot. Everything is carried out with military precision and an attention to detail I have learned the hard way.

Only when I'm sure everything is in place; do I leave for work.

On the dot of eight every morning, I lock the door and make my way to my car parked in the drive. I could probably do this in my sleep because it's a routine I've perfected for the last five years.

As I join the traffic, nothing changes. I swear the same cars accompany me on my journey to the office and yet I couldn't tell you the make or model.

The same radio station provides the only life in the car because mine ended five years ago.

As I turn into Gander Green lane, my heart starts racing. I start to feel anxious because what if *she's* not there?

I've come to rely on the stranger who provides the only light in my life.

8.15 and I feel my heart thump as the latest single to top the charts plays loudly from the radio.

I feel the anxiety that always follows me as I count the houses. Three doors down from the pub and the little white gate will open.

It starts to rain and the wipers squeak across the windscreen as I strain to see.

I start to slow down to prolong the encounter.

As I reach the second house, the flash of red I catch in the corner of my eye settles my heart.

There she is. The woman who has come to mean so much to me. The only one who settles my nerves and makes me feel almost human.

As I hold my breath, she starts the gentle jog towards me. The rain makes no difference to her. She dresses accordingly and even the little black dog who trots by her side is dressed for the elements.

She is laughing at something and grins as the little dog starts to bark at a cat across the road. I feel my world right itself as she pulls the dog along and smiles happily.

Just a split second is all it takes for me to imagine myself in her place. Happy and free without a care in the world. A pretty house and a faithful companion. Surely that's not much to ask, is it?

The memory will keep me company for the rest of the day. It makes sense of my life and gives me hope of a better future. Sad really, when the only bit of happiness I enjoy is through the eyes of another.

The song finishes and the presenter starts talking about their next guest. I turn the radio off. Now my only companion is the imaginary world I create as I imagine myself walking in the girl on Gander Green lanes shoes. I want to be that woman so badly it hurts. I wonder where it all went so badly wrong.

Just before nine, I reach the office in town where I've worked for the past three years. As I join the line of workers pressing through the doors I hear, "Morning, Sarah."

I say on autopilot. "Hi, Bea, terrible weather out there."

"Yes, it's going to last most of the week, unfortunately."

I smile as I walk past the beaming receptionist.

Faville and Proctor - the Insurance company where I work and the only place I can relax.

Most of the people here dread coming in each day. I don't.

Most people call in sick as many times as they can get away with. I don't.

Most people moan about the management and the workload they inflict on us. I don't.

I would stay here if I could because what waits for me at home is far worse. There I'm on edge and here I can relax knowing that I won't have to explain myself and deal with the consequences.

As I take up my position at the desk fourth from the door and facing the window, I feel myself sigh with relief as I switch my mind to the day ahead.

5.30 comes all too soon and with a heavy heart, I join my co-workers on the commute home.

I don't dawdle and chat as many do. Any invitation to the pub after work is politely declined. I smile regretfully and make up some excuse to extricate me from any 'out of office' plans. I need to be home by 6.30 and have everything in place because that's what's required of me.

The return journey is much the same save for one thing. The girl never appears. She must work or walk her dog another time because as hard as I look, I never see her.

As I pass, I look with interest at the house she lives in. It's a pretty house with roses trailing over a white painted porch and the garden is worthy of any horticultural accolade. Although welcoming, it's not pristine. The gate could use a coat of paint and the path is strewn with weeds. However, the plants that grow in the small garden take my breath away.

It looks a happy house where nothing bad ever happens and once again, I wonder about her life. I imagine she has everything she could wish for. A beautiful home and no worries. She is obviously happy; I can tell that by the smile on her face. She has a lightness to her step which shows a confidence that only a happy life can give you.

As usual, I refuse to dwell on my life. I deal with it on a need to basis and the less I think of it the better. As I leave Gander Green lane behind, I leave my heart there to collect the next morning.

When I turn into Richmond Avenue, the houses change and the street widens. The trees stand proudly, guarding the neighbourhood like soldiers. The houses are bigger, better and much more impressive. Behind the shutters are people who live their lives in a very different way. People that appear to have it all worked out and look down on those who don't. Doctors, lawyers, businessmen and their cosseted families. Nothing bad happens in Richmond Avenue - nothing that is spoken about, anyway.

Sighing, I turn into the drive of number 15 and pull up in my usual parking space. I turn the key in the ignition and hear the birds singing outside.

Then I take a deep breath and head inside the place that has been more like a prison than a home for the last five years because this is where *he* lives.

CHAPTER TWO

You can do 99 things for someone and all they'll remember is the one thing you didn't do. – unknown

I quickly shower and change and set about making supper. As I pull the fresh ingredients from the fridge, I concentrate on the task in hand. Lasagne with a green salad and the usual bottle of wine. I work quickly and methodically making sure nothing is left uncleared or out of place.

I work in silence and channel my energy into making the food because the rest of the evening will be spent living on a knife edge.

I hear the car turn into the driveway and my heart starts racing. The thump of the car door and the sound of footsteps and my nerves jangle. The sound of the key in the lock strikes fear in my heart as I wonder what mood will be coming through it today.

Then I hear those footsteps heading my way and I plaster a smile on my face and say, "How was your day, darling?"

I watch as my husband heads my way and don't miss the way he takes everything in.

Richard Standon is an impressive-looking man. He is good looking and dresses as if he's just walked out of a men's magazine. His hair is dark and cut short and his eyes are the darkest I have ever seen. He keeps himself in shape and we head to the gym most evenings. During the day he works as a solicitor and earns more per hour than I do for the day. Many of the women we associate with want to be in my shoes. He is easily the best looking of the husbands around here and I'm aware of the jealous looks and envious words as they constantly tell me how lucky I am.

He heads towards me and pulls me close, whispering, "I've missed you today."

I answer as he would expect. "Me too."

Pulling back, he strokes my cheek lightly and says softly, "What do you say we leave the gym tonight for a different type of workout?"

He asks me a question that demands no answer and I smile softly, "I would like that."

He runs his hands down the front of my dress and says in a voice that gives me chills. "I expect you dressed accordingly at 8 o'clock sharp."

Nodding, I lower my eyes and he pulls away saying roughly, "What's for supper?"

My heart flutters as I say shakily, "Lasagne and salad."

He sighs irritably. "Again?"

I say nothing and he rips his tie off angrily. "For god's sake, Sarah, what was the point of that course I sent you on if you can't even rustle up something more interesting than a lasagne. You're a waste of space, you know that?"

I used to feel upset when he spoke to me like this but I'm so used to it I say nothing and just turn to carry on with my work.

He heads off to change and I close my mind to anything other than getting through the night.

He returns just as I'm dishing up and I pass him a glass of his favourite wine and say dutifully, "How was your day?"

He shrugs. "Same old routine. You know, I was thinking we should take a holiday. Maybe head to the Caribbean to get away from it all. I'll book it tomorrow."

I swallow hard and try to look excited. "That would be amazing. Let me know the dates and I'll book the time off."

He sighs irritably. "I've been thinking about your job. I think it's time to leave. We need to start thinking about a family now. I'm not having my wife working when she should be concentrating on raising our family."

I feel light headed as I try the dodge this conversation that is becoming more regular as the weeks go on.

"When were you thinking of going?"

He groans. "It will have to be next month because my workload is too heavy. Leave it with me and I'll sort it out."

I try to look excited but my heart is sinking like a lead balloon.

As usual, Richard eats with one eye on the television and I'm grateful for it. At least if he's concentrating on that I'm off the hook. The thought of going on holiday fills me with dread. Two weeks with him and no escape. Most women would love the chance to escape to a Caribbean island with a man who looks like him. I'm not one of them. They don't see the man I see behind closed doors. The man who wants everything his own way and demands more than a woman should ever have to give. To everyone else, we have a perfect life. I disagree. The woman I want to be lives on Gander Green lane and if I could turn back the clock, I would do everything in my power not to have fallen for the man before me.

After supper, Richard retires to the couch to watch the television, leaving me to clear the dishes and straighten the kitchen.

I make him a coffee and head across the large, open plan room, that you could eat your food off the floor.

As I hand him the mug, he says darkly, "Wait."

My heart starts thumping as he places the mug on the coffee table and sits back in the chair. He fixes me with a hungry look and says gruffly, "Show me how much you've missed me."

Swallowing hard, my hand moves to the zipper on my dress and as it falls, I stare him in the eye and note the lust enter them. I move forward and straddle him on the couch as he runs his hands all over my body making me shiver inside. Lowering my lips to his, he kisses me in a hard-demanding way before saying roughly, "Go and wait for me."

I offer him a long, lingering, kiss and sway sexily from the room. My heart beats so fast I can only pray it gives out on me because sex with Richard is not straightforward. He has particular tastes that don't sit well with me and yet many other women would consider me lucky.

As I lie on the bed and wait, I try to focus my mind on anything other than what's happening.

He makes me wait for one hour.

I hear the television playing loudly in the room downstairs. The telephone rings and I hear him laugh at something in the conversation. I feel cold but dare not climb under the covers just in case. The air conditioning blasts its cool air on my nearly naked body and numbs me to what I'm about to receive.

My teeth are chattering when he finally enters the room. Fully dressed with intent in his eyes. I watch as he removes the belt from his jeans and his eyes flash.

"You've been a naughty girl, Sarah."

My heart starts racing and my voice trembles as I say fearfully, "I'm not sure what you mean."

His voice is ominous, and he says darkly, "I found this down the side of the couch."

He produces a letter and I start to shake. My mouth is dry and I say in a whisper, "I'm sorry."

There's no point in denying it, it would only make matters worse. The letter I hid was one from my old school. It's a reunion that's been arranged for one month from today. Richard's key was in the

17

lock before I could hide it. It arrived two days ago, and I forgot about it completely.

He pulls the letter from the envelope and reads it out in a dull voice.

Then he crumples it into a ball and advances towards me slowly. "Why didn't you tell me you were going to meet up with your past?"

I say softly, "I wasn't going to go. I wanted to throw it in the trash before you got home."

His eyes flash. "Are you sure about that, Sarah, you see I don't believe you. I think you were going to go without me and that makes me angry."

I start to shake as he winds the belt around his fist and says angrily, "Why would you hide something like that unless you were planning something? You know I don't like secrets and it makes me mad. I'm thinking the worst now, Sarah because maybe there's a secret you don't want me finding out. Is that the case because if you're hiding something from me, I won't be happy?"

He reaches the bed and stares down at me and I shake my head. "I'm sorry, Richard. I never mentioned it because I didn't want to go. I thought you may make me and they are the last people I ever want to see again."

He removes his shirt and I see the lust shining in his eyes. "You know I believe you, don't you baby? You know I trust you, don't you?"

I swallow hard and say weakly, "Yes."

Shaking his head, he sits astride me and says softly, "You know this will hurt me more than you, my darling."

The tears fall from the corners of my eyes as I nod and say in a whisper, "Yes."

His breathing becomes more ragged and I steel myself for his punishment.

Flipping me over, he reaches across and tethers my hands to the metal bed frame with his belt. I feel the bite of the leather as it tears at my skin as he kicks my legs apart. Running his hand down my back, he says in a sinister voice. "You only have yourself to blame for this. You know I love you, don't you?"

I say in a whisper, "Yes."

His hand runs over my ass and pinches it hard. Then he says roughly, "Do you have anything to say?"

My voice sounds far away as I say shakily, "I'm sorry, Richard, please forgive me."

He hisses, "For what?"

"For keeping something from you and hiding the evidence."

As soon as the last word leaves my lips, his hand connects with my ass. The pain shoots through me and I bite my lip. I feel the sting as he says, "Tell me you love me."

Squeezing my eyes tightly shut, I say, "I love you, Richard."

Slap.

Another stinging blow makes me cry out, and he says angrily, "Did you just make a sound?"

Slap.

Another stinging blow as I shake my head and then he says darkly, "You know I have to punish you, don't you, Sarah?"

I choke out, "Yes."

Slap.

This time the blow is even harder and catches me on the part that still smarts from the previous one. I bite my lip as he says, "I don't think you're sorry enough."

I start to plead. "Please Richard. I'm so sorry. Please forgive me."

Slap.

The tears fall and it feels as if I'm fire. Then I hear the sound of his zipper and feel him enter me roughly, cruelly and without care. He starts to pound into me from behind as the pain fills my mind. His grunts are the only sounds in the room along with the bang of the metal headboard against the wall as he punishes me. He is relentless until he satisfies himself before pulling out.

The cool air on my abused ass soothes the pain as I hear him move to the bathroom. I lie still and make no sound as he cleans himself up before returning what is probably 15 minutes later. His voice is laced with derision as he says slowly, "What do you say, Sarah?"

I whisper, "Thank you, Richard."

He reaches for the belt and unties my hands. Then he pulls me to face him and wipes the tears from my eyes with his fingers.

"Why do you push me, baby? You know what it does to me."

He pulls me towards him and holds me in his arms rocking me like a baby.

"There, there, it's over now, all is forgiven."

He pulls me against him and we lie in the darkened room until sleep erases the horror of my reality. Sleep is the only escape from this living hell and I'm not sure how much longer I can go on.

Chapter Three

We could never learn to be brave and patient, if there were only joy in the world. Helen Keller

Life carries on as normal the next day and I'm just grateful for the chance to see the girl I want to be having a happy life. As I drive to work, I imagine myself in her shoes. How lucky she is to wake up every day with no fear. I expect she has many friends and a loving family. She probably enjoys a loving relationship without fear and looks forward to going home every night.

I'm not sure how my life ended up this way. When I first met Richard, he was everything I hoped for and more. I used to feel so incredibly lucky that he chose me and I suppose it's that part of me that didn't stand up for myself when it started. I should have seen the warning signs. I should have known, but I was always so afraid he would leave me. Now I want that more than anything. Ironic really.

The weekend comes and signifies an end to any freedom I enjoy. We wake at 7 am on Saturday morning and the first item on the agenda is our usual jog around the neighbourhood. I make sure to follow Richard a few steps behind so he can set the pace. Despite everything, I love this morning jog. It means I can grab some alone time without the need for conversation.

Richard listens to his music and sets off at quite a pace. I am not allowed that luxury because my job is to act as his eyes and ears for approaching cars. As we turn the corner, I see Sally Benson heading towards her car. She is dressed for her usual Pilates class and she raises a hand to wave and I see Richard acknowledge her. I do the same and she calls out, "See you later guys."

Nodding, I leave her behind and think about the evening ahead. It's the usual monthly get together with the neighbours. Tonight, it's at Sally and Crispin's home and promises to be the usual assault course as I attempt to navigate through an evening where I pretend we are a normal and happy couple.

I see James Clyde washing his car and Richard raises his hand and waves. I just smile across the street and see him grin and shake his head as he carries on with his task.

Mrs Barlow's dog barks as we pass her front lawn and the paperboy ahead crawls along the kerb, throwing the papers on the driveways as we pass.

As days go, it's going to be a good one. Weather-wise that is. The sun is already promising a glorious summer's day and the sweet birdsong should fill me with happiness. The trouble is, nothing does anymore.

I'm not sure when I stopped loving Richard. It was so gradual it shocked me when the realisation hit. I think back over the last few years and feel so incredibly sad. I was so happy when Richard started paying me attention. We met through friends and I

23

remember wondering how on earth such a man was still single? He was attentive, funny and kind and I fell in love with him almost immediately.

I suppose we had what's called a whirlwind romance and within six months we were engaged and planning our wedding. We married on a beach in Antigua and the fairy tale was all set for a happy ever after.

Maybe it's because I have such low self-esteem, I placed him high above me on a pedestal. He could do no wrong and I had to up my game if I stood any chance of holding onto him.

You see, our whole relationship was filled with anxiety from the start. I was afraid of losing him so let the odd cruel comment slide. They started coming more often, and he caught me out on many things I had done wrong. The burnt dinner as I chatted on the phone. The birthday card I forgot to post and the childhood trophy I smashed into pieces by accident. I began to think I was clumsy because whatever I did ended badly. His pristine white shirts dyed pink from a top of mine caught in the wash. Shredding a valuable document by accident and leaving water marks on the polished furniture. It was always my fault, and I deserved the cutting remarks and character slurs.

However, I didn't. Nobody deserves to be made to feel as worthless as I do. In the early days, I challenged him. There were many raised voices and terrible arguments that lasted for days. Sex was the only way out of them and it's that part of me I hate the most. The part that craves his touch and longs for his approval. As I said, he's an impressive man, and any attention was worth more than no attention.

Soon he started to dominate me in every way. He started to control every part of my life, starting in the bedroom. At first, it was fun to play games and try different things. Then it spilled over to our everyday life and now he controls every part of me 24/7.

I feel disgusted with the whole situation. I hate myself for becoming this weak-willed woman, with no backbone to fight back like I know I should. As I said before, to everyone else I have it all. I wish I could just walk away because I would rather have nothing than this tainted life of mine.

We reach home and my heart sinks as Richard says over his shoulder, "I'm taking a shower. Make sure you tidy up before you have yours."

He kicks off his trainers and heads upstairs, leaving me to put them in the laundry room to be cleaned and put away.

Out of the corner of my eye, I see the postman deliver the mail next door and head outside to see what he's got for us. However, when I check the mailbox on the wall outside, it's empty which strikes me as odd. It has been for the last few days which is unusual. There is always post, whether it's a circular or a bill, there's always something.

I see Gloria my neighbour and she waves and says brightly, "Hey, Sarah. Still sticking to the regime, I see."

Looking down at my running vest covered in perspiration, I smile. "Yes, it's good for you. Maybe you should try it."

She laughs loudly. "Listen, honey. I have the fittest personal trainer in the world who visits me at home three times a week. Let's just say he pushes me hard and I need the remaining days to recover."

She winks as she grabs her mail. "You know, I could get you his number if you like. I can highly recommend him."

Shaking my head, I roll my eyes. "No thanks, I have more than enough to keep me busy."

She laughs. "I should say so. You hit the jackpot with Richard you lucky girl. Anyway, it's at least eight hours before we're due at Sally's. I need to get ready."

Her laughter floats across the manicured lawn, framed by sweet smelling, herbaceous borders. As I look around, it strikes me that Richmond Avenue is impressive. There is nothing out of place and it almost looks like a film set. Even the flowers looked staged. The woodwork is pristine and mainly painted white. The grass is cut about an inch all over and the concrete clean and free from weeds or marks.

Nothing about life in Richmond Avenue seems real. Pretty houses and fancy cars sit proudly outside. Any children around these parts are well behaved and kept mainly indoors. It doesn't seem normal and I wonder when this perfection started to disturb me. As I think of Gander Green lane, my heart settles a little. Nothing is perfect there but everything *is* perfect. To me, anyway.

As soon as I get inside, I place my soaked running clothes in the laundry basket and wrap myself in my robe ready to shower. As I head upstairs, I have to pass through the dressing room to reach the shower. I see Richard with a towel wrapped around his waist while towel drying his hair. He straightens up and I hate the way my body reacts to the sight of him. It betrays me every time and is the main reason why I'm as weak as I am.

Trying to distract him, I say with surprise. "You know, Richard, we haven't had any mail in days. It's unusual, do you think something's happened?"

He looks up and shrugs. "I had it redirected."

A cold feeling creeps through me and I stutter, "What do you mean?"

He shakes his head and says angrily, "I set up a redirection to the office. After that little stunt you pulled the other day, I can't trust you to be honest about what arrives here. This way, I get to check that nothing is being kept from me."

My heart starts thumping, and I say shakily, "You can't do that. It's against the law to tamper with mail."

He looks at me furiously and I start to shake inside as he crosses the small room quickly and grabs my wrist hard. He says coldly, "You have made me into this person, Sarah and if you don't like it, you only have yourself to blame. I need to be able to trust my wife and here I am having to monitor your every move because you keep on hiding things from me."

His grip is biting into my wrist and I try to pull away which angers him more.

He pulls me roughly against him and grabs hold of my hair, pulling it tight. Then he snarls, "You will get your mail when I get home at night. You can open it yourself in front of me and then we will have no secrets. I am saving you from yourself and you need to understand that everything I do is with your best interests in mind. So, what do you say, Sarah?"

I say fearfully, "Thank you, Richard."

He pushes me away and I stumble against the wall. My wrists hurt and the tears well up in my eyes. Richard just carries on getting ready and says dismissively, "You need to shower; I can smell you from here."

Quickly, I head to the shower and close the door, hoping he leaves me to it. There are no locks on the doors in this house, he saw to that. I have no privacy at all and he walks in unannounced even when I'm using the toilet with no regard for privacy. Consequently, I don't hang around and make short work of washing the sweat and fear from my body, before grabbing the robe from the hook on the door.

When I enter the dressing room, I'm happy to see he has left and I sit on the bench, shaking. I shouldn't be surprised about the mail. In fact, I should be more surprised that he didn't think of it sooner.

Once again, I wonder how much longer I can go on. I need to get away from here and fast but I have nowhere to go. My family have made it clear they want no part of my life and any friends I had before have long since faded away. Richard didn't like them and made it difficult for me to see them. The only friends we have are the neighbours and his office colleagues. I have no money because he controls all the bank accounts and gives me a small amount each week for the necessities. The credit cards are in his name and even my wages get paid into his account. My phone is on a contract with his and my car is in his name.

It's always just been easier to get through the day and hope things change. The worse thing is, I fantasise about him having an accident on the way home from work. The sight of a police car at my door would fill me with happiness rather than sorrow. Sad really, when the only way out is to wish him to die.

The rest of the day is spent like every other Saturday. I clean the house from top to bottom and Richard hides away in his study. Occasionally, he ventures out to check my work by running a finger along a door frame or pointing out some dust in the corner that has escaped the hoover.

I make us lunch and we sit together at the table overlooking the street, while he tells me why everybody who lives here is beneath us.

It's almost with a sigh of relief that I get ready to head out to Sally's house for the evening. At least we will be among company and can pretend we're normal just like everyone else.

Chapter Four

Jealousy, that dragon which slays love under the pretence of keeping it alive. Havelock Ellis

Sally and Crispin live in a large, white, house, similar to ours. As soon as we knock on the door, it swings open and Sally yells, "Here they are, my favourite neighbours."

She says this to everyone, so we smile politely and hand her the bottle of wine we brought with us. Crispin slaps Richard on the back and says loudly, "Good to see you, come and get a beer."

I watch with relief as he drags Richard off and Sally links her arm in mine. "That's got rid of them. Come on, I'll fill your glass full tonight, honey, you look as if you need it."

I can't argue with that and allow her to pull me among the other wives who are sitting in the garden enjoying the last of the day's sunshine.

I take a seat among them and go through the motions of pretending everything's alright. Gloria leans over and whispers, "Hey, you see Angela over there."

I look across and see one of the other neighbours looking a little worse for alcohol already.

She says in a low tone, "Word is, Vincent's having an affair with their nanny. Not very original but apparently Angela caught them when she came home early from Yoga."

I say in a shocked voice, "That's terrible, what did she do?"

Gloria shakes her head. "Took to the bottle – again."

"What about the nanny?"

Gloria sneers. "Still there. You know Angela. The thought of her husband having it away with the hired help is just an inconvenience because if she had to actually look after her own children, she would be in rehab quicker than she could uncork the next bottle."

I stare at Angela in amazement and say sadly, "The poor woman."

Gloria snorts. "Don't feel sorry for her, honey. She told me she was enjoying playing with her new pool boy. They're as bad as each other and will never change. What's the point in staying married when they obviously can't stand each other?"

My heart flutters and I try to look as normal as possible. "Yes, why indeed?"

I catch Richard's eye and he smiles sexily across the room, making Gloria sigh beside me. "On the other hand, there's the two of you. Love's young dream and the envy of us bored housewives everywhere. You're the lucky one, Sarah. You give hope to the rest of us."

I bite my tongue because she couldn't be further from the truth. The trouble is, Richard has perfected the happy couple routine over the years. He is attentive, caring and kind in company and the complete opposite when the door closes on the world. Nobody would believe me if I told them what really went on behind the closed doors.

It must be about thirty minutes later, we hear someone tapping a glass and calling for hush. I look in surprise as James Clyde says loudly, "Attention everyone, Jenny and I have an announcement to make."

Gloria says in a low voice, "No prizes for guessing what this is all about."

My heart sinks as I sense another battle heading my way if this is what I think it is.

James puts his arm around his wife and beams proudly. "We heard a few days ago we'll be welcoming a new addition to our family in eight months' time. Jenny and I are pregnant."

Gloria snorts loudly and luckily the noise of congratulations drowns it out, as everyone adds their voices to their neighbours in congratulating the proud couple. I daren't look but catch Richard's eye and my heart sinks. He looks determined and I know where this is heading.

I try to shake the ominous feeling aside and join the others wishing our friends luck and happiness for their future. A little later, I get a moment with Jenny and smile at her happily. "I'm so happy for you both."

She positively beams. "I can't believe it, Sarah. We've been trying for so long and had so many failed attempts I thought it was never going to happen. It just goes to show you should never give up."

She looks across at Richard and sighs. "I wish you would join us. Just think of the babies you'd have with a husband looking like that. We could share in the whole baby experience and our children would grow up together and be best friends."

My heart sinks. The thought of bringing children into my volatile world isn't worth thinking about. I know Richard is keen to start a family and I've always managed to dodge the issue. However, by the look on his face, my time is up.

He heads across and kisses Jenny on the cheek. "Congratulations. You will make wonderful parents."

Jenny blushes prettily and I roll my eyes to myself. They all adore Richard and think I'm the luckiest woman alive. If only they knew.

James heads over and kisses her lovingly which makes me happy for her. Richard takes my hand and laughs softly. "You know, James. I think you'll make a great father. Maybe Sarah and I should join you and we could compare notes."

They look at us with excitement and Jenny says, "I'd love that. I was only just saying as much to Sarah."

Richard pulls me to his side and says with determination. "We've been thinking of it for a while now and I don't think we should put it off any longer. We could certainly have a lot of fun practicing."

They all laugh and I smile politely but inside I'm dying a slow death. Not if I have anything to do with it.

The rest of the evening is spent discussing the new baby and I feel as if the walls are closing in on me.

By the time we say our farewells, I'm a nervous wreck.

Richard almost pulls me over in his haste to get home and my heart sinks as I sense another battle ahead.

As soon as we get inside, he races upstairs and I follow with trepidation. Then I watch in disbelief as he heads to my bedside drawer and empties the contents on the bed. He grabs all the packets of birth control I have and starts emptying them down the sink. Racing over, I pull on his arm and shout slightly hysterically, "Stop, what are you doing?"

He pushes me away and says darkly, "No more, Sarah. We've talked about this long enough. All the time you take protection you are denying me what I want the most. It's your duty as my wife to provide me with a family and I'm putting my foot down."

I feel the hysteria pushing away my better judgement and scream, "Stop, you don't have the right to make my decision for me."

He pushes me away sharply and I fall onto the bed and he shouts, "Enough. You will do as I say and no arguments. You've had long enough to come to terms with this and my patience has worn out."

I watch with desperation as he flushes every last pill down the sink and then looks at me darkly. "Don't think about ordering any more because I will find out. From now on you will be available whenever I call until my baby is inside you."

He kneels on the bed and pushes me roughly down. His hand presses against my throat as he snarls, "How do you think I feel when all around me my friends are proving their manhood? It's embarrassing when I see the pity in their eyes when once again it's not us making the announcement? They probably think I'm not up to it, firing blanks and not able to give my wife what she desires. Well, not anymore. This time I'm insisting you do your duty and be the mother I want you to be."

The tears slide from the corners of my eyes as he pulls me close and whispers, "You know I'm right, don't you, baby. I know you're scared but you don't have to be. You'll be the perfect mother as you are the perfect wife. I love you so much and want nothing more than to see my baby swelling your belly. I want everyone to see the love I have for you growing inside you. We will make wonderful babies darling and our lives will be complete. First thing on Monday morning you will hand in your notice at work. Then we will make sure you build yourself up with vitamins and rest to increase your chances of falling pregnant. I'll be with you every step of the way my darling and you don't have to worry about a thing."

I feel his hand inch up my leg under my dress. He starts to stroke me through my panties and rubs his thumb against the thin silky material. Groaning, he shifts and pushes the thin fabric aside before pushing his own pants down. Then, with one hand holding me down, he enters me slowly and deliberately. He thrusts hard and fast and growls. "I will make a woman of you, Sarah, just don't challenge me. You know I love you and this is for your own good."

I say nothing as he takes what he wants. There's no point in resisting, it would only make things worse. Once again, I despise myself as I lie back and let him use me without putting up a fight. This is a sick and twisted marriage and it's up to me to end it. The trouble is, I don't know how?

Chapter Five

They always say time changes things, but you actually have to change them yourself. Andy Warhol

I'm not sure I slept a wink all night. I lie like a statue beside Richard who slept like the baby he so desires.

Everything was rushing through my head and making no sense at all. I know I have to act because the last thing I want is a child with the monster who occupies my bed. Little did I know that the monster under my childhood bed would turn into the husband that shares it in my adult life.

I think I explore every possibility as I count down every hour to morning. I know there are places for women to go who need to escape. I even researched them one day from work in my lunch hour. It scares me to think it's my only possible path and worry about what that would mean. I would have to go far from here and start again, but with what? I have no money and even my passport and driving licence are kept at Richard's office in case of a fire at home. I have allowed myself to be controlled 100% and have nobody to blame but myself.

Even if I went to the police who would believe me? Richard makes sure he never leaves a mark on my body and I have never told anyone about what he does - I couldn't, I'd be too ashamed. Richard's a solicitor and could argue against the best of them. He would turn it around and put the blame on me. I need to be clever and work things out properly because I need to know I'll be successful. But time is running out because I know if he gets his way, I'll be pregnant within the month.

Sunday comes and with it, Richard's parents. As if the weekend hasn't gone badly enough, Sylvia and Mason arrive like a bad winter.

I've always hated his parents. They have never thought I was good enough for their son and have made that pretty clear over the years.

I watch as they all greet each other affectionately and smile politely as they turn their attention to me.

Richard says shortly, "Sarah, take mum's coat and fix them a drink. They shouldn't have to wait."

Swallowing hard, I nod and say apologetically, "Of course, I'm sorry. Please, let me take your coats. What drinks would you like?"

Sylvia smiles thinly. "A white wine for me and Mason's usual beer."

She turns away, effectively demoting me to the usual role of the hired help and starts to question Richard about work. I'm actually happy not to be included. Their company bores me and I'm happier when I'm left on my own, anyway.

I make myself look busy and try not to listen to their conversation. All I can think of is the need to get as far away from here as possible but a sudden shriek gets my attention.

"Richard, that's fantastic news."

I feel their eyes on me and say with surprise, "Sorry, what news?"

Richard laughs softly. "There's my scatterbrain. I was just telling mum and dad about our plans to start a family."

My heart sinks as Sylvia says loudly, "Not before time. It's been a long time coming and I must say, I thought you'd chosen a woman who couldn't reproduce for a moment there Richard."

They all laugh and then look at me accusingly. Mason says, "Good for you. If it's a boy, I'll put his name down at the club. It's a long waiting list so he should be near the top when he's 21."

They all laugh and I cringe as I see the life my poor child would have with them as its family.

Richard laughs loudly. "Yes, it's long overdue. Don't worry though, Sarah is going to hand in her notice tomorrow and become a stay at home wife. Maybe you could give her a few tips mum?"

Sylvia nods. "Of course, it would be my pleasure. I will teach Sarah everything I know and by the time I've finished with her, she will be the perfect wife and mother."

I can feel them all staring and say faintly, "I'll check on the lunch."

My eyes swim with tears as I picture my life. I can't let this happen; it will destroy me.

As I try to take a few deep breaths, Richard comes behind me and says softly, "See, everyone agrees. This is the next step to our perfect life. Just remember, it's all for you, baby. I want to give you the life you deserve and we will grow old together. You know I'll never let you go, don't you?"

His words chill my heart and I daren't turn around because he would see it in my eyes. His voice lowers, and he says darkly, "Remember, I control you for your own good. Don't challenge me and everything will be ok."

I hear his mother call, "Remember we are on a strict vegan diet now."

I grit my teeth as I stir a pot of the deepest, richest, beef casserole. Richard turns and says irritably, "Since when?"

His mum laughs in embarrassment. "Since we watched a programme on where our food comes from. Honestly Richard, you would turn vegan if you saw it."

I feel the pressure building in my head as Richard snarls, "Honestly, Sarah. You should have thought to check if they had any particular dietary requirements. Dinner is now ruined and I blame you for this."

The tears prick my eyes and I feel like hitting him with the bloody dinner. I take a deep breath and say lightly, "I'm sorry, we didn't know, Sylvia. Maybe we should all head out for lunch instead. There's a new restaurant in town that the neighbours have been raving about."

She shakes her head. "Well, I must say I'm not really interested in going out. I would have thought you had something in reserve for people who don't eat meat. Maybe you could rustle up a salad or something. I'm sure that cookery course Richard paid for you to go on at great expense must have taught you something."

Biting my sharp retort, I just say with resignation, "Leave it with me, I'll see what I can do."

I'm not sure how but I manage to rustle up something that passes as a vegan meal and we sit down around an hour later. Sylvia makes a great show of picking at her food and turning her nose up, saying dully, "It's a bit bland, isn't it?"

Richard looks annoyed and Mason, to his credit, a little embarrassed. He catches my eye a couple of times and smiles apologetically but wouldn't dare comment. I'm starting to see where Richard gets his personality because Sylvia is a monster. I wonder if Mason has a difficult life and suffers like me in his own way.

As they talk, I tune out and go through the motions. Their visit can't end soon enough for me and I watch the clock which appears to be running slow because it never seems to move.

They must have been here for about four hours before they get up to leave and Richard takes my hand and we stand to say our goodbyes.

I watch Sylvia's eyes mist over as she kisses him lightly on the cheek. "It's been lovely to see you, son. Remember to visit us soon and I'll make sure to serve your favourite food. You look as if you need looking after and there's nobody better than your mother."

She looks at me and nods. "Goodbye, Sarah. I'll search for some vegan recipes for your folder. It's an area you could use some brushing up on."

Richard nudges me as I say, "Thank you, Sylvia, you are very kind."

Once again, Mason smiles and looks embarrassed but he still says nothing. Seeing him standing beside Sylvia so meekly, reminds me of myself. Will that be me in the future? A life spent biting my tongue and agreeing with everything Richard says. I already know it is because I am that woman now. Wearily, I wave them off and turn to clear up the mess their visit has made.

Richard sees them to their car and then heads back and I jump as he slams the door. "Well, that was a disaster. What do you have to say for yourself?"

I say with resignation. "Sorry Richard."

He shouts angrily, "You always are. Sorry should be your middle name. How did you not know they were vegan? When was the last time you called my mother to check on her? Have you ever shown any interest in their lives or tried to get to know them? Well, we both know the answer to that, it's no. You are just so wrapped up in your selfish life you don't even try anymore."

I feel my legs shaking as I try to diffuse the situation. When Richard loses his temper, there can only be one outcome – a terrible evening ahead for me.

"I'm sorry, darling, you're right. I'll make more of an effort."

My words seem to do the trick and he sighs heavily. "This just cements our decision. First thing tomorrow, you will quit your job and spend your days perfecting being a wife and then mother. You can't do both and your work is seriously impacting on our relationship. I'll go and draft the letter now and you can take it in tomorrow."

He leaves the room and I lean against the sink with relief. At least he didn't touch me. Maybe he will forget and get distracted by the television or some work he usually does in the evening. All I can do is carry on clearing up and plan my escape because now I'm more certain than ever. I'm leaving Richard and I'm leaving him very soon.

Chapter Six

If you're going through hell, keep going. Winston Churchill

The sun is shining and the birds are singing in the trees. The day is fresh and promising and as I make my way to my car; I feel optimistic. The letter in my hand reminds me of urgent business and I feel my heart racing wildly as I make a decision. It's time to fight back.

I see Gloria as I back the car from the drive. She raises her hand and I smile happily. All around me the residents of Richmond Avenue go about their normal routine and I am no exception. However, today I am not going to the office. Today I am going to get the help I should have got years ago.

As I drive along the familiar roads, I feel a spark of hope sitting alongside me. I can do this; I am a strong woman. There is no need to suffer in silence in anymore. There are people trained to help with situations like mine and I shouldn't be afraid to ask for help.

As I turn left into Gander Green lane, I feel my world right itself. The familiar street that I associate with freedom calls out to me as I travel along it. There is no radio to distract me today, just my own thoughts that won't be silenced anymore.

As I reach the gate of the third house, I hold my breath. My heart lifts as I see the girl close the gate behind her and start her gentle jog. Then something happens that takes me by surprise. Something different that has never happened before and something that makes my decision all the more certain.

She looks me in the eye as I pass and smiles brightly.

Just a brief moment but the connection was clear. She actually smiled at me. I didn't even have time to smile back before I moved past her but I will never forget the kindness reflected in those eyes.

I find myself smiling as I carry on with my journey. Instead of turning right out of Gander Green lane, I turn left today. Instead of the mind-numbing journey to Faville and Proctor, I pass along unfamiliar streets that will take me to a different destination. The place I am heading signifies freedom and understanding. No appointments are needed, just a bit of bravery and a firm resolve.

As I pull into a space in the car park, I feel my heart thumping and the nerves setting in. One step is all it will take to free me from my prison. One person to hear me speak who will make everything alright.

Just for a moment, I sit in silence. This is a huge step for me and I'm acting on impulse which may not be a good idea. However, I know I don't have long. Richard is getting more demanding, and the violence is starting to scare me. What started out as a little fun has escalated into abuse and I don't want any part of it. It's this thought that helps me make my decision. I need to face my fears and deal with this for both our sakes.

As I leave the car, my heart thumps with every step I take. I walk towards the civic hall and pray they can help me. There's a support group that runs from here where women can go to for help. I am that woman and just hope this doesn't backfire on me.

Every step I take is a positive one. That's what I need to tell myself because if I don't hang onto that thought, I'm liable to think twice about my decision.

As I reach the entrance, I can feel my heart beating madly inside me. Then, as I place one hand on the door, I hear a loud, "Is that you, Sarah?"

I feel the blood drain from my face as I stiffen and turn to face the person behind the voice.

I see my neighbour Angela heading towards me with a smile and frantically think of a reason why I'm here.

She rushes over and says breathlessly, "I thought that was you. What are you doing here?"

Such a simple question but I don't have an answer, so I just shrug "I need to order a new bin. Ours is falling apart."

She nods sympathetically. "I know what you mean. I could do with a new one myself. It's good to see you though, do you have time for a coffee?"

Swallowing hard, I shake my head regretfully. "Not really, I should be at work and lost track of the time."

She smiles ruefully. "Oh well, maybe next time."

I say curiously, "What brings you here?"

"I help out once a week at a group here. I volunteer as my way of giving something back."

Trying to sound normal, I say with interest, "Oh, what group's that?"

She lowers her voice and looks serious. "A woman's refuge. You know, the stories I hear would break your heart. Normal women who are treated appallingly by their husbands and partners. I'm not going to lie; it makes me so mad."

Feeling my heart sink, I say softly, "And do you… help them, I mean?"

She nods. "Oh yes. These women are largely afraid and have nowhere else to go. We put them in touch with professionals who offer them a way out. I must say, I love what we do here, it really makes a difference you know."

Then she laughs loudly, "Lucky for us we don't have such a burden to bear. Our husbands are the real deal and I thank my lucky stars I found Vincent. Can you imagine how awful it would be to live in fear?"

Feeling my hopes dissolve into dust around me, I smile sadly, "No, I can't imagine."

Angela smiles. "Anyway, I should really get inside. Mondays are usually busy after the weekend. I'm not sure why but that always seems the catalyst to make up the women's minds. I expect we will be busy today."

As she turns to leave, I say with a slight edge to my voice, "Oh, Angela, please don't mention you saw me here today."

She looks confused. "Why ever not?"

I roll my eyes and laugh. "If Richard found out I was here, it would make life difficult. I told him I'd ordered this bin weeks ago, and he's been struggling with the old one wondering why it's taking so long. I don't want him to be annoyed."

She smiles. "Don't worry. I know what men can be like. I'm always telling Vincent I've sorted things I totally forgot about. Don't worry, your secret's safe with me."

She winks as she turns away and I wait until she disappears inside before quickly heading back to my car. As I fasten my seatbelt, I feel the ever-present tears behind my eyes as I see my way out of this nightmare slipping away. I can't possibly go to them for help now. Angela would know about it in a second. I'm not stupid enough to allow my secret to be exposed to somebody who knows us, it would be all around the neighbourhood in seconds. This is a disaster and I'll need a Plan B if I am to ever free myself from this marriage.

So, with a sigh, I start the drive to work to deal with the next problem.

Luckily, I am only five minutes late, which is a miracle considering the traffic problems this time of day usually brings. Wearily, I park the car and head towards the office, the resignation letter burning a hole in my pocket. The last thing I want to do is give up the one piece of freedom I have left but I'm not stupid enough to think I have a choice.

Gloomily, I sit at my desk and stare sadly out of the window. How did my life spiral out of control this fast? When did I lose my backbone and why did I allow it to happen?

"Hey, Sarah, did you hear the news?"

I turn in the direction of the voice and see Jane who sits beside me leaning over, looking excited.

She whispers, "Word is we've been bought out. There's a meeting later on today and the rumour flying around is there are redundancies on the cards."

I say with interest, "How do you know?"

She looks around and whispers excitedly, "I overheard some guys talking in the elevator this morning. Apparently, we're to get an email later on today and to be honest, this couldn't have come at a better time for me."

"Why?"

"I've got another job lined up as a receptionist for Hammond and Rogers, the Insurance company across town. If I hang on, hopefully I'll get the redundancy and a nice cheque to send me on my way."

The phone rings and she turns her attention back to work and I feel a tiny spark of hope ignite inside me. What if it's true? Maybe this could be my way out. I've worked here long enough to know that if I took redundancy I'd be due a large pay out. Maybe this could be my lifeline. I could opt to be paid by cheque and Richard would never know. I could set up a bank account of my own and use the money to disappear. Maybe this is fate giving me a way out.

I almost can't concentrate on my work and feel my heart thumping to the beat of change and new beginnings.

A shadow falls across my desk and I look up into the kind eyes of the floor manager, Mr Jenkins. He smiles reassuringly and nods towards his office. "May I have a word, Sarah?"

I nod in surprise and follow him to the office at the end of the room, wondering what this could be. Maybe it's linked to Jane's conversation from earlier.

He gestures to the seat in front of his desk and I perch on the edge nervously. As he sits down to face me, I see a flash of uncertainty cross his eyes as he says softly. "I'm sorry to drag you away from your work but I needed a private word."

Squirming on my seat, I wonder if this is because I was five minutes late. Maybe I should have come and apologised but the look on his face is one of compassion rather than anger, so I just smile shakily.

He sighs heavily and says wearily. "I'm not sure if you've heard the rumour flying around but things are set to change here very soon. We've been taken over by Grant & Miller and things are up in the air at the moment to say the least."

I look at him with a worried expression. "What will happen?"

He shrugs and shakes his head. "Nothing for now but I'm told we're looking at shed loads of redundancies while we merge with the new mother ship. It may not affect this department but then again, it may affect us all. We will be living with that uncertainty for a while until the dust settles."

He smiles ruefully. "Anyway, that is kind of why I called you in."

I lean forward and look at him expectantly as he smiles. "I understand you were going to resign today."

The shock must show on my face because he smiles reassuringly and says softly, "Your husband called this morning and briefed me on what to expect. He told me you were nervous and may take a while to pluck up the courage."

His words are like a jagged knife tearing my heart out as I try to look at him with a normal expression but my heart is thumping close to critical. He smiles again. "I told Richard about the possible redundancy and it has changed everything. We both agreed it's best for you to hang tight until we know for sure. That way you will get the pay-out you deserve which will help with the new family."

I feel dizzy as I croak, "New family?"

He stares at me keenly and I feel myself blush as he says gently, "It's ok, Richard told me about your... um… situation. He's worried about you and told me the reasons for your departure."

I barely manage to get the words out as I say weakly, "Situation?"

Shuffling forward on his seat, he lowers his voice still further. "Don't worry, Sarah. I am most discreet. Richard told me you were struggling and your mental health was suffering. I just want to reassure you that as soon as you start taking it easy, Nature will bless you with the child you so desire. My own situation is not dissimilar to yours. It took us years to conceive and my wife was much the same as you. Frantic and obsessed with having a child. Well, it was only when she gave up hope altogether and turned to look at adopting that she fell pregnant naturally. I must say, you are lucky to have such a supportive husband. He is concerned for you and wanted to remove all the stress in your life, hence the resignation. Well, I think I've convinced him to hold fire for a few weeks to see where this all takes us. In the meantime, I am reducing your workload to help with your stress issues. You will now be responsible for incoming calls only and can pass any of your cases to Sandra and Michael to deal with."

He leans back looking pleased with himself while the screams start in my mind. I say shakily, "Richard called you?"

I can't seem to get past that and the walls close in on me as I realise my fragile escape plan has once again been cruelly taken from me.

He smiles. "Yes, luckily, we know each other by association, so he felt comfortable calling me and speaking confidentially on this sensitive matter."

I say weakly, "You know Richard."

"Yes, he works for the organisation my wife heads up across town. They support victims of domestic abuse and Richards' company provide legal assistance. He's been an invaluable asset to her organisation which is why I'm keen to repay the favour. Don't worry, Sarah, we will get through this together and you can rest assured, I will take all the worry away from you and liaise directly with your husband. We just want what's best for you and hopefully you will soon have the family you deserve."

He looks at me kindly and I feel my world imploding all around me. How does Richard do this? He is everywhere and whatever road I think will take me out of this hell, he has already set the road block in place. Even the people who are there to help women like me have been blindfolded by him. This is a disaster and there's nothing I can do about it.

My legs are like lead as they carry me from Mr Jenkin's office. I walk past my desk and head to the restroom for some much-needed privacy. As I sit alone in the cubicle, I place my head in my hands and the tears fall freely. I make no sound as those tears wash away all the hope I had left. My future is no longer mine to control. How can I when all of my choices have already been made for me? Even if

I did manage to find somebody to believe me, they would be powerless to help - wouldn't they?

Chapter Seven

How much more grievous are the consequences of anger than the causes of it. Marcus Aurelius

Somehow, I get through the day. After all, it's something I excel at. Disguising my pain and appearing as if life is normal. Maybe that's been the problem. Perhaps I should have told somebody sooner and they would be able to back up my story. I'm not stupid enough to think that if I went to the police, they would believe me, anyway. Richard is too clever for that.

Increasingly I am aware he has covered every base. His abuse is more mental than physical. In company, he appears the perfect husband and charms his way into their hearts. In private, he controls, manipulates and abuses without leaving any physical marks. He has covered his tracks and fabricated a story of my mental fragility and it's only now I can see the full picture. Richard has sealed my prison shut with a carefully constructed web of lies and deceptive imagery and I can't find the end of it to unravel. The only way out is to fight my way out and he has made sure I don't have the strength for it. Now I'm to produce him a family which will cement me by his side forever. This is it, the end of the line. Match point and checkmate because Richard has won. I can see that now, there's nothing else for it – I must bow to the inevitable and do what he wants. My life is now effectively over.

There was no announcement forthcoming by the end of the day, so we were left to return home with uncertainty an unwelcome passenger.

My journey along Gander Green lane is a different one to earlier. At least then I had a small shred of hope that things may change for the better. Now, as I move past the little white house, all I can see is a hellish future married to the devil himself. The sight of the pretty house brings tears to my eyes. How I wish I was that woman who appears to have it all. I'm guessing that the life behind those drapes is a very different one to mine, it's obvious by the spring in her step and the happiness that shines from her like a light in a storm.

Happiness, I had that once. I had that feeling that followed me through life where everything was perfect and the future looked bright. I couldn't believe my luck when I found Richard. He complimented my life which was rich and full of friends and laughter. One by one those friends drifted away. I wanted to please him and he dominated my time. Any invitations were declined for a much better offer from him. I couldn't get enough of his attention and turned my back on everyone but him. It didn't matter. I had everything I ever wanted – my soulmate.

I wonder where those friends are now? Maybe I could look them up and seek their help. Maybe they would be the ones to steer my ship through the rocky sea. With a sinking feeling, I realise I don't know how to find them. Their numbers have been lost over the years and I'm not stupid enough to look for them on social media. I'm not allowed it anyway and Richard checks my phone every night for any browsing history.

I wrack my brains to remember any small shred of information that may help me. Perhaps I should start talking. Tell my neighbours. The paperboy, the postman, in fact, anyone who will listen. Surely, I could start sowing the seeds of my situation with anyone who will listen. I have that chance at least.

These thoughts and many more accompany me home. I can't give up without a fight because even if it means losing everything, it will be a price worth paying for freedom.

Richard's angry.

I can tell by the way the whole house shakes as he slams the front door. I feel the fear creeping over me as his footsteps head towards me.

My heart thumps with every sound of his approaching mood. My head starts spinning as he stands in the doorway and snarls, "Do you have anything to tell me, Sarah?"

Swallowing hard, I feel the dry taste of defeat on my tongue as I say in a small voice. "No."

His words fly across the room like imaginary bullets as he snarls, "Where were you today?"

Frantically, I think of every excuse under the sun as I realise he must know about my visit to the council offices.

He says darkly, "I'm waiting."

Turning away, I say in a small voice. "I went to work."

In two strides, he cuts across the room and grabs my wrist, shaking me angrily.

"Then how do you explain the extra mileage on your car?"

My heart sinks and I stutter, "I was distracted and took the wrong turn."

I should have just told him the story I told Angela because he shouts, "Liar. Do you take me for a fool, Sarah?"

I start to shake and say with a quivering voice. "No."

His grip is like iron as he pulls me from the room towards the stairs. I stumble as he pulls me roughly up them and towards the room at the end. My knees shake as I plead, "Please, no, Richard. I promise you; I'm telling the truth."

He says nothing and carries on pulling me towards the door at the end. The tears blind me as he kicks the door open and pulls me into the room I hate the most. The punishment room.

There is no light in the punishment room. The shutters are always closed with blackout blinds cutting out every sliver of light.

There are no frills or finery in the punishment room.

Dark, oppressive walls, painted to serve a sinister purpose. Fear.

One single metal-framed bed, sits by the wall with just a mattress and nothing else. A bucket sits by the side of it and the floor is made up of bare boards. I start to shiver as I plead, "Please don't do this, Richard."

He snarls angrily, "Strip."

I start to cry gently, "Please, no."

He says harshly, "Take your punishment, Sarah and no more will be said. You know I don't like it when you lie to me."

Sobbing, I remove my clothes and he says darkly, "Now lie on the bed."

I try one last time. "I'm sorry, Richard, please forgive me."

He laughs dully. "You want forgiveness, well, you have to earn it. My patience is starting to wear thin with you, Sarah. All I want is a wife who does what she's told. I provide a loving home with everything you could ever want and this is what I'm rewarded with. A wife who skulks around in the shadows and hides everything from me. A wife who shows no interest in my family and starting one of her own. A wife who sits meekly in company and yet challenges me in private. You need to learn the hard way what being a good wife involves and it pains me to be the one to teach you."

I start to cry and he says in disgust. "Look at you kneeling on the floor stripped of your dignity. Snivelling like a chastised child when you can see you have no way of dodging your lies. They will always betray you, Sarah, because you're just not clever enough. You see, I will always win because I'm always ten steps ahead of you. You think you're smart hiding things from me, which only shows how stupid you really are. You know, I could have had anyone but I chose you. I still could because I'm considered quite a catch. You, on the other hand, would only attract the flies because that's what you are, Sarah, you're filth. A filthy, dirty, liar who deserves nothing but the back of my hand and a night to think about how you can make it up to me."

Grabbing my hair, he twists my head sharply and says angrily, "Get on the bed."

I do as he says and lie face down. I sob as he ties my wrists and ankles to the bedposts and feel the bite of the rope, just tight enough to secure but leave no marks. Then, he places a blindfold around my eyes and I hear him say darkly, "What do you say, Sarah?"

I sob. "I'm sorry, Richard"

The silence is more frightening than the knowledge of what's coming. My heart beating frantically is the only sound I hear as I wait for him to strike.

Slap.

The first blow causes me to cry out as I feel the sting on my ass and he grabs my hair and pulls back sharply, hissing, "Did you just make a sound, Sarah?"

Shaking my head, the tears soak the blindfold as he releases me and then I feel him gag me with a rough piece of material and I steel myself for the next blow.

A few minutes pass and then.

Slap

This time I stay silent and try to tune out the horror happening right now.

Slap

Slap

Slap

Slap

Slap

I bite down on the gag and taste the blood in my mouth. The metallic, rancid taste of my own weakness as I take what he gives me.

The door slams and I hear the key turn in the lock.

He's gone.

Chapter Eight

Keep your face to the sunshine and you cannot see a shadow. Helen Keller

I start to shiver. There is no heat in the punishment room. The air conditioning rains down an icy blast cooling the heat from my punishment. The cold air dries my tears and cakes the blood that drips down the side of my mouth.

There is no sound in the punishment room. Soundproofed walls cut out reality and enhance the fear in the room. I can't hear him come until he arrives. There is no life apparent in the punishment room because any sounds have been muted and banished from the real world.

I can't move in the punishment room. Tethered to the bed I lie like an animal, stripped of all humanity. Alone to think about what brought me here and acting as a deterrent for the future. Obey my husband and master. That is the lesson learned here. It's simple. Do whatever he says and sacrifice my soul to him. Never speak out and agree to everything he wants.

I feel the numbness setting in. It surrounds my heart like an icy glove and squeezes it hard. It freezes my hopes and dreams and renders me incapable of decisions. It strips away any fight left in me and harnesses my mind to his.

Time has no meaning in the punishment room. There is no light to signify the hour, and no sounds to dictate if it is night or day. I have been known to spend several days chained to this bed lying in my own excrement as I 'think about what I've done'.

Sleep doesn't come easily in the punishment room. There are too many thoughts to process. Too many things racing around my head and too much fear to leave my senses unguarded.

The only thing that's good about the punishment room is that I'm alone.

I drift in and out of sleep and the cool air wakes me every time. My teeth chatter and my body feels numb. My limbs ache from being held in the same position and my shame is intensified as I wet the bed which, for a brief moment, provides the only warmth in the room. The cool air dries it on my leg and the smell makes me gag. I can't move and my joints scream out in frustration and pain. No more tears fall because they dried up a long time ago along with my resolve. I am broken. I have been for some time. Every time I think I can free myself; something happens to drag me back down. This is no exception.

I'm not sure how long I lie here for. Hours, days, weeks, time has no meaning here.

Then the sound of the door opening causes my heart to quicken. I hear him approach the bed and snarl, "This room reeks of you, Sarah. A disgusting putrid smell of weakness and a meaningless life. Have you learned your lesson?"

I nod and he removes the gag from my mouth. My mouth feels dry and my lips cracked as he says harshly, "What do you say, Sarah."

I whisper, "Please forgive me, Richard. I'm sorry."

The bed sags as he sits beside me and strokes my hair. "Good girl. You have earned a sip of water."

He grabs me by the hair and pulls my head back and holds a glass of cool water to my lips. I drink greedily, desperately and with gratitude as the cool liquid calms the desert in my body.

He strokes my back and moves his hands over my smarting ass, saying darkly, "You know it pains me to see you like this, Sarah. I don't enjoy bringing you in line but you will challenge me in every way. So, do you agree that I know best?"

"Yes."

"Do you agree that I have only your best interests at heart?"

"Yes."

"Do you promise to obey me and do everything I say?"

"Yes."

"Will you be the good wife and mother I deserve?"

"Yes."

He removes the blindfold and says soothingly, "There. That wasn't so bad was it?"

I say in a whisper, "No."

He strokes my body like a favourite pet and groans.

"Look at you, baby. So beautiful and all mine."

I say nothing as he loosens the ropes around my ankles and massages the life back to them.

He says softly, "Does that feel good, baby?"

I nod. "Yes, thank you."

He releases my wrists and pulls me to face him and strokes my face. "Look at you. Everything a man could ever wish for. I love you so much, darling, you know that, don't you?"

I nod, willing a smile to my lips. "I do."

I feel his hands on my breasts and hear his breathing intensify.

"We will make beautiful babies my love. We will be the perfect family and I will give you the world."

I smile weakly. "Thank you, Richard."

I feel his fingers move down my body and feel them entering me. He groans, "Feel how much you desire me, Sarah. Your body betrays you every time."

The shame washes over me and I hate myself more than him at this moment. Is it possible to despise someone, yet still crave them physically?

His eyes darken and he pulls me from the bed saying gruffly, "Clean yourself up and I will reward you in the bedroom. You can clear this mess up afterwards."

Meekly, I follow him from the room as he leads me to the bathroom where he has filled the tub with sweet smelling, hot water, surrounded by candles.

I step inside and he joins me, pulling me back against his chest as he washes my shame away. He kisses my neck and whispers, "I love you, darling. Now I will show you what my love can do."

He kisses my neck, nibbling as he goes. His hands move across my breasts, squeezing gently and causing them to stand to attention.

The warm water causes my mind and body to relax as he lifts me from the tub and carries me to our bed.

Richard is a good lover when he wants to be. Tonight, he is proving that over and over again. He knows how to work my body until it betrays my own feelings. It's a whore to Richard because it demands his attention. It exists only to please him and he plays it like a fine instrument, coaxing it to do his bidding and chaining me to him forever.

Richard makes love like he makes hate. Skilfully, controlling and causing every thought in me to agree with him. This time, I am encouraged to cry out. This time, my cries are ones of passion and ecstasy. This time, my heart beats a different tune as I draw him inside me, craving what he gives me. When the high wears off, I will come crashing down. I will loathe myself as well as him. I am ruined forever by this man in every way. I am lost with no map to aid my way out of a bad situation. I am broken.

Chapter Nine

*I've learned that fear limits you and your vision.
It serves as blinders to what may be just a few steps
down the road for you. The journey is valuable, but
believing in your talents, your abilities, and your
self-worth can empower you to walk down an even
brighter path. Transforming fear into freedom - how
great is that? Soledad O'Brien*

Life goes on. Meaningless, controlled and
unforgiving life. Surrounded by riches and yet
nothing is inside. My life, my world, my shame.

Then one night everything changes.

The door slams and I jump as usual. He's home.
A little earlier than usual which makes the hairs
stand up on the back of my neck as I wait to see
what mood comes through that door today. To my
knowledge, there is no reason for him to be angry. I
have been the model wife since my punishment. I
have run the home like a well-oiled machine.
Played my part well as his loving wife and gone to
work and spoken to no one. Even when we've met
up with the neighbours, I've smiled and joked with
them as usual and gazed at my husband lovingly in
public. I've even made an effort with his mother,
albeit through gritted teeth. I phone her regularly
and ask for tips on recipes and household remedies.

I jump as Richard flings his briefcase to the floor and says loudly. "Evening, Sarah. We don't have long, so I expect my supper on the table within the hour because we're going out."

I say with surprise. "Where to?"

Shaking his head, he rips off his tie and says irritably. "Where you tried not to go."

I look at him in confusion and he rolls his eyes. "Don't be obtuse, Sarah. Remember the letter you received that made me so angry?"

My heart lurches. "Yes."

He smiles darkly, "The reunion. Tonight, we are going to see just what you're hiding from me. I will delve into your past and you had better pray there are no deep, dark, secrets you're hiding because I will find out and you know how angry I get when you hide things from me."

My knees start trembling and I lean on the kitchen counter for support as I whisper, "Why?"

He shrugs. "Because I don't like secrets where it concerns you. There was a reason you hid that letter from me and it has made me curious. So, tonight we will revisit your old school and you can introduce me to your friends. Maybe they will shed some light on the past you are so keen to protect."

He heads toward me and I shrink back in fear which makes him laugh dully. "It appears I was right to be concerned. The fear is evident in your eyes. Is there something you want to tell me before we go?"

I shake my head and he sighs heavily. "I'm off to change and I expect supper on the table when I return. Don't make me angry because I am feeling unsettled. Work has been hard lately, added in with the worry about you. I'm not sure why we're still not pregnant and that makes me wonder if you have kept to your end of the bargain."

Shaking my head vigorously, I almost shout, "I promise I haven't taken anything. How could I, you flushed the pills away?"

He raises his eyes and says angrily, "I'm not sure I can trust you. You like your secrets and this may just be another. You had better pray for a miracle soon because my patience is running out."

He heads off leaving me shaking. Why is he doing this? I've done everything he asked and more. There hasn't been a night gone by where he hasn't expected me to do my 'duty', as he puts it. I haven't complained and if I'm not pregnant yet, it's not because of anything I've done. Maybe I can't have children, that would actually be a blessing in disguise. Maybe he can't provide them, a fact that would be the best kind of payback. The fact I'm so stressed probably has a lot to do with it as I wait for the inevitable to happen and seal my fate forever.

We eat in silence as my stomach churns thinking of the evening ahead. This is a disaster. I know what will happen. Past friends will reminisce about old times. Bring up old misdemeanours and past boyfriends. Richard will charm the stories from them which they will only be too happy to spill.

When he wants to, Richard can be the most charming man on earth. It's why he's such a good solicitor. People tell him things they shouldn't and I will pay the price. I was certainly no Angel at school. I had my usual share of parties and guys I dated. I'm pretty sure Richard won't like any of the stories from my past and that's what scares me the most. Whatever he hears will send him into a rage when we return. I may as well accept that my stay in the punishment room will be a lengthy one because he is not going to like what he hears one bit.

I dress conservatively and his eyes gleam as I join him downstairs. He pulls me close and says huskily, "You look amazing, baby. When you make the effort, it reminds me of why I fell in love with you."

He runs his fingers around my waist and says with longing, "I hope your underwear is as impressive because I am going to enjoy ripping it off you later."

The predatory look he throws me sickens me. Not his look, I'm used to that but the ever-present longing that shoots through me when he directs that gaze at me. I know Richard desires me. It's evident by the way he looks at me. The trouble is, it sickens me because I am no different. Whatever this relationship is that we share it's twisted because I loathe and love him in equal measures. I desire him and he repulses me and I could kill him but would mourn the loss. My head is screwed and there is no way back because I am a ruined woman.

We take my car because Richard informed me his was low on petrol. It makes no difference because what we arrive there in is of no consequence. As I sit meekly beside him, he says irritably, "I don't know how you can live with yourself. This car is a mess. Look at the smears on the windscreen and I saw some dirt on the mat. The seat is too far forward, and it smells of stale air and your inadequacy."

I say nothing, there's no point. It would only serve to anger him prior to our evening and there will be more than enough there to stoke the flames of my looming punishment.

As the radio plays, he sneers, "I told you only to listen to classical music. This music is of no benefit whatsoever. How on earth are you expected to raise my children when you listen to trash like this?"

He turns the station to his usual classical one and the haunting music plays through the speakers, loud and spellbinding.

The light has gone and the darkness of night has set in. The headlights pick out the shadows of the familiar as we pass by.

My heart starts thumping as we head towards Gander Green lane. Tonight, I can take a lingering look at the house that holds all the answers to me and stare into the window before they close the curtains on the night. We turn into the street and

Richard says suddenly. "I heard from Mr Jenkins today."

My mind snaps to attention as he says airily, "Your redundancy has come through and your last day will be Friday. They'll be paying the money straight into our joint account, so don't go getting any ideas."

I hold my breath as I stutter, "What do you mean?"

He laughs. "I know how your mind works and if I know my stuff, you were hoping to keep that money for yourself. I'm not an idiot, Sarah. I know you're planning on leaving me and I won't have it. You can plot and plan all you like but I will never let you go. We are married, and that's forever in my book. If you leave, I will find you and the fact I have to go to so much trouble to control you shows me how unstable you really are."

I'm not sure why but something snaps inside me. Maybe this is the last straw of many, or maybe it's because I'm in the street I feel at home in but I shout, "How dare you!"

There's a sudden silence in the car and I feel the red mist descending as I shout, "Five years I've put up with you. Five years you've worn me down and made my life a misery. I've done everything you've ever asked of me and more and what do I get? I get a fucked-up husband who thinks this is a marriage. Well, it's not, it's a dictatorship. It's a world with no forgiveness. You have belittled me, bullied me and made me into a shadow of my former self. I've done everything you've ever asked of me and it's still not good enough. Well, I've had enough. Do you hear that Richard, enough? You can stick your marriage and perfect life where the sun doesn't shine because I want a divorce."

It happens so quickly I don't have time to react. I feel the stinging blow knock my head against the window as Richard punches me hard in the face. My vision blurs as I hear him yell, "You don't get to talk to me like that. I own you, Sarah and that will never change. You will never divorce me because I would rather kill you first."

I'm not sure what happens next because everything happens so quickly. A flash of yellow draws my attention as I see the little gate open. Then a shape runs out into the road and I scream. "Richard, look out!"

I watch in horror as the little dog's frightened eyes are caught in our headlights as we bear down on him. Then I hear myself scream as a larger shape follows him. The sound of the brakes screeching adds to my screams. I see her looking me straight in the eye as we hit. I stare at the woman who means so much to me, as the car hits her body and propels it over the windscreen. My cries are drowned out by the sound of metal crunching and the radio blaring. The car hits something and pushes me forward and my head hits the screen and I feel a sudden pain as the glass breaks and shatters all around me. There is a smell of fuel and the sound of pain mingled with shock.

For a moment I am blinded by a light and then there is silence.

Chapter Ten

Anger is an acid that can do more harm to the vessel in which it is stored than to anything on which it is poured. Mark Twain

My heart races out of control as I make to exit the car. A hand reaches out and grabs hold of my arm and Richard screams, "You stupid bitch, look what you've done."

I look around and stare at him in horror. Blood is dripping from his head onto my hand and he pulls me to him and screams. "You did this, you, Sarah. You've caused this accident and you're taking the blame."

I stare at him in shock and then in the light from the headlights, I make out a shape slumped on the ground outside. I gasp and struggle to free myself, screaming, "What have you done?"

He yells, "You did this, remember, it was you. You've killed that woman and will pay the ultimate price."

I break free and race to the still shape on the ground. Sobs wrack my body as I rush to her side. There is blood everywhere and I sink to my knees and scream. "Help us, please, help us."

I hold the woman in my arms and my tears fall onto her lifeless body. She looks so serene and peaceful. There isn't a mark on her, yet the blood runs through my hands like Satan's river. I stroke her head and say desperately, "Please come back to me. I'm so sorry. Please, don't die."

I don't even register that anybody else is there, as my world crumbles and my blood drips onto the woman whose life I have taken in one foolish moment of anger.

I feel hands pulling me away and lash out. "Don't touch me."

Then a firm voice says, "It's ok, help is on its way."

I cry, "Please help her."

Two strong arms lift me away from the battered body at my feet and pull me into a hard chest. Strong arms wrap around me as a voice says, "Don't look. You're in shock, the ambulance is on its way."

I hear the sirens and struggle to break free. I start to sob, saying wildly, "I'm so sorry, it's Richard, we didn't mean it, it's an accident. Oh god, I can't bear it, I'm so sorry."

I feel those arms hold me in place as they shield my eyes from seeing what's happening. A soft, strong, voice soothes me, saying, "Everything will be fine. You'll be fine, I've got you."

I'm not sure what happens next because then there is nothing.

I wake in a hospital bed with a police officer on either side of it. My head hurts so badly and my eyes feel heavy and sore. I hear one of them call the nurse and then I see a kind face staring at me. "It's ok, Sarah, you're in the hospital. You've been involved in a nasty accident but you're going to be ok."

My mouth feels dry and I manage to croak, "Richard... where's Richard?"

The nurse shakes her head and looks at the police officer who leans forward. "Is Richard your husband Sarah?"

I nod and then remembering the girl, cry out, "What happened to the girl, is she ok?"

I watch them share a look and the nurse shakes her head slightly. I feel my heart thumping as she says, "Just rest now. All will be explained after you have some rest."

I can tell by the look on their faces it's bad and my heart sinks like a stone. Turning to look at the police officer on my left, I say desperately, "Please tell me, is she.... dead?"

His face tells me everything I need to know and the sobs wrack my body as I realise what we've done. A brief moment of madness has caused someone to die. I can't see for the tears and hear the nurse say angrily, "I'll get the doctor."

I'm not sure how long the doctor takes but he soon arrives and I hear a kind voice say softly, "It's ok, Sarah. I'm going to give you something to help you sleep."

I barely register the needle grazing my skin before blissful oblivion claims me to a place where nothing can reach me.

When I wake, it doesn't take long for the memories to re-surface. Shaking my head, I open my eyes and see the weary police officers slumped in their seats beside me. One of them notices me waking and leans forward. "Shall I call the nurse, Sarah?"

Swallowing is difficult, so I nod and he leaves the room, returning seconds later with the same nurse. She smiles warmly and says brightly, "I'm guessing you could use a nice cup of tea. Let me organise it for you and make you more comfortable."

She works around the officers who just watch with blank expressions on their faces. I suppose it's then it strikes me. Why are they here?

By the time I'm sitting up and feeling a little more in the land of the living, I look at them with many questions waiting for answers. The first one I have to ask is, "Please, tell me about the girl, is she ok?"

They share a look and then one of them says softly, "I'm sorry, she didn't make it."

The pain hits me like a lightning strike and the tears fall quickly and trickle down my face as I realise what we've done. The officer says gently, "Can you remember anything about that night?"

I nod miserably and he takes out his notebook and says kindly, "Do you want to tell us?"

I make to speak as the door opens and the doctor heads inside the room. He looks at the officers angrily and says shortly, "Please leave. I need to examine my patient."

They make to protest but the doctor isn't having it. "I said, now!"

With resigned looks, the officers leave, and the doctor says angrily, "I'm sorry, Sarah. You need to know what happened but you also need to heal. I must examine your wounds and talk to you about their implications."

For the first time since the accident, I think about myself. My hand reaches up and I touch my head where the pain is constant and say fearfully, "What happened to me?"

The doctor smiles kindly. "You took a blow to the head that may have happened on impact. The windscreen shattered and several pieces of glass embedded themselves in your skull, narrowly missing your eye. Your body sustained multiple bruising, and you broke three of your ribs. We've taken a scan and everything appears fine but you'll probably be sore for a few weeks while your body heals."

I shake my head and say sadly, "Is that it? A few cuts and bruises and a few broken bones. Not much of a punishment for ending another's life, is it?"

The doctor shares a look with the nurse and says softly. "You don't have to say anything without a lawyer present. The police are here for answers but you do have rights."

A lone tear trickles from my eyes as I say almost as an afterthought. "What about Richard, my husband?"

Once again, they share a look and the doctor says carefully, "We are trying to locate him but he isn't answering any of his calls."

I look at him in surprise. "What, he isn't here?"

Their looks are starting to worry me and I say slightly hysterically, "Where is he?"

The doctor takes my hand and squeezes it reassuringly. "We don't know. We've left a message and I'm sure as soon as he finds out you're here, he'll be racing to your side."

A knock on the door interrupts things and the doctor sighs as the policeman pokes his head around the door. "I'm sorry but we need to question Sarah if she's up to it."

They all look at me and I say sadly, "Of course, I'll help as much as I can."

The doctor says firmly, "Ten minutes and if she gets agitated, you must leave immediately."

They leave us to it and I say fearfully, "Where's my husband?"

The police officer sits beside me and says blankly, "We had hoped you could tell us that."

I shake my head and sigh heavily. "The last I saw of him was at the accident. I left him in the car and went to help the girl. The next thing I knew, I woke up here."

There's a brief moment of silence and then the officer says, "Are you saying your husband was with you in the car?"

I nod miserably. "He was driving."

I look into his eyes and something about his expression tells me I'm not going to like what I'm about to hear. I almost can't get the words out but have to know, "Is he... dead?"

The officer looks down and then up again, saying darkly, "Sarah, there was nobody else in the car with you. You were the driver and we have witnesses who will swear an oath to that effect."

I stare at him in disbelief. "What witnesses? I swear Richard was driving."

The officer shakes his head. "Your husband is missing, Sarah. I am afraid to tell you we are treating his disappearance seriously because when we searched your home, we found evidence that he has been seriously hurt."

My head is spinning and I say fearfully, "What do you mean... missing?"

The other officer speaks up and says in a hard voice. "It appears that something happened at your home on that fateful night. A search revealed blood stains on the walls synonymous with a fight. There were broken tables and ornaments and blood was smeared all over the walls as if someone fell and scraped down them. That blood is an identical match to Richard Standon, who we believe to be your husband. We have also analysed the clothes you were brought in wearing and that blood matches the type found on your coat. Do you remember what happened because, by the looks of things, you were fleeing from the scene when you hit an innocent pedestrian?"

I hear the words but they don't make sense and stutter, "That's a lie. That never happened. I promise you, Richard was driving."

The other officer says kindly, "Then tell us in your own words what really happened that night, Sarah."

I hold my face in my hands and say with a trembling voice, "We were going to my school reunion. We argued, and I told Richard I wanted a divorce. He got angry and punched me hard in the face and the next thing I knew, I saw a little dog on the road. I called out and then *she* appeared."

I break off and start to cry as the silence hangs in the air waiting for the conclusion. Then I whisper, "She ran into the road and I screamed. The next thing I knew, the car hit her and threw her up in the air. She bounced into the road and we crashed. I tried to go to her but Richard pulled me back and told me I would pay for the accident. I never listened and ran to the girl. The next thing I knew, I was here."

The officers share a look and then one of them says, "We will need to take a full statement at the station. As soon as you are discharged, we will arrange for a solicitor to be present and you will be interviewed."

He stands and heads to the door, saying over his shoulder, "I'll organise your discharge."

As he leaves the room, I say fearfully, "Am I in trouble?"

The officer nods gently, "I'm sorry, Sarah, but it looks as if you are to be charged with causing death by dangerous driving and the possible manslaughter of your husband."

As his words sink in, I pass out.

Chapter Eleven

I used to think that the worst thing in life was to end up alone. It's not. The worst thing in life is to end up with people who make you feel alone. Robin Williams

It's been two days since my life unravelled. I was discharged and taken into custody. The police officers arranged for a solicitor and I was interviewed for hours but we got no further forward than what I could tell them. All the time, I kept on thinking of the girl. Her name is Ellie Matthews. Now she has a name and isn't just the girl on Gander Green lane. A young woman whose life was cruelly extinguished in a moment of madness. She had so much to live for and everything going for her and we took that away.

I know the police officers don't believe me. I tried to tell them what happened, but it started to sound a lie even to my own ears the more they twisted the story.

It was on the third day I broke.

"I'm sorry, Sarah, but we are getting nowhere. You have told us what happened yet the facts don't add up. Your husband is missing and if what you say is true, he fled the scene of the accident unseen when we have several witnesses who saw you at the wheel and swear you were alone. He is then supposed to have run injured back to your home and fabricated a fight before disappearing off the face of the earth."

I stare at him with tired eyes and nod. "I can't explain it, officer. I've told you what happened."

The officer's share a look and Detective Inspector Jones sighs heavily. "Why did you want a divorce, Sarah?"

There it is. The one question that threatens to unravel the perfect life we created. Now is my chance to get everything out in the open but it's hard. Can I really voice the words that I've hidden for so long?

My solicitor smiles at me with encouragement and the tears fill my eyes as I whisper, "He hurt me."

The room stills and there is no sound as they wait for me to continue. The tears blind my eyes as I begin the sad and bitter tale of a marriage that went so badly wrong. I leave nothing out and once I start, I can't stop. The memories are raw, painful and vivid and yet it's as though I'm talking of somebody else.

As soon as I finish, there is an awkward silence in the room and DI Jones says wearily, "So, you are telling us this has been going on for five years and you never once told anyone about it."

I nod, ashamed of myself.

He leans forward and says in a hard voice. "I'm sorry, Sarah, your story doesn't add up. There is no evidence to back up what you say and in fact, any statements we have, tell a completely different story. You were the perfect couple. Your husband idolised you and gave you everything you could wish for. He cared for you and was in fact, concerned for your mental health."

My head snaps up and I look at him in disbelief as he continues. "I have sworn statements from your boss and several neighbours that say he was concerned about your state of mind when you struggled to conceive. You became withdrawn and depressed and he was afraid you would do something to harm yourself. He spoke to them about the arguments you had as he begged you to seek help. Apparently, he was scared to leave you alone because he wasn't sure what he would find when he returned. You see, Sarah. Your husband, on several times, sought help for your problems but it appears you did not."

I shake my head and whisper, "He's lying."

The officers share a look and I can tell they don't believe me, so I say desperately, "I can prove it."

Leaning forward, officer Coleman says kindly, "How can you prove it?"

Stealing a look at my solicitor, I say quickly, "There's a room."

They look confused and I say with a tremor to my voice, "The punishment room."

I feel the memory searing my soul as the tears fall. "He used to lock me in there when I upset him. Sometimes for days. I was tied to the bed, blindfolded and naked while he punished me."

The solicitor reaches out and squeezes my hand and looks compassionate but the officers do not.

DI Jones says, "Where is this room?"

I sob. "In the house on the top floor."

He leans forward. "Then maybe you should show us."

I look at him in fear and yet know I have to go back. They have to know and have to believe me, otherwise, Richard will have won.

The other officer, PC Coleman, stands and says curtly, "I'll arrange it."

Coming home feels wrong. Richmond Avenue is different somehow. It stands as if it's waiting for something to happen. It is empty and still and as the police car turns into it, I feel the hidden stares and the eerie silence of a street waiting and watching. There is no life left in this street as we come to a stop outside number 15.

I swallow hard as I look up at the house I once lived. It was never my home because I hated every minute I was in there. I'm not sure what I feel about it now. It looks cold and dispassionate and I wonder if it's rational to hate a house for what went on inside.

Even the birds stop singing as we take the short walk up the driveway. I see the police tape preventing entrance, warning of a situation inside. The officer takes my door key from his pocket and it feels strange entering a place I lived with two strangers beside me and another behind.

As we step inside the hall, I smell the scent of home. A strange mix of sandalwood and citrus courtesy of the polish we used to use. Everything is always neatly arranged for fear of Richard's temper because he liked to live in an orderly fashion with nothing out of place.

The house looks the same but then I see the plastic covering on the floor. As we walk into the large, open plan, living space, I feel the scrutiny of the police officers who are watching my every move.

I gasp as I look around at the devastation of a once perfect space.

What appears to be blood decorates the white painted wall and the furniture is lying on its side, broken and ruined. Photo frames are shattered with the photos inside looking up from the floor like ghosts of a former life. Plants spill on the floor, their earth burying shards of glass. It looks as if a huge fight happened here and my mind spins out of control as I wonder what happened.

I think I already know because Richard is a man who plans everything down to the last detail. He is responsible for this because he told me I would pay. This is his revenge for me daring to speak out against him. This is my punishment because I'm not stupid. Richard has set me up and is probably hiding out somewhere waiting for me to be convicted. Knowing him, he has already started again. A new identity, a new life and no trail to follow. I always knew he was dangerous, but this is something else entirely.

Officer Coleman says gently, "What happened here, Sarah?"

I whisper, "I don't know. I told you what happened. This must have been Richard's work. He must have returned here and made it look as if we had an argument. I swear it wasn't like this when we left."

The solicitor rubs my shoulders and I'm grateful for the small amount of kindness she shows me. Maybe somebody believes me because I'm fast realising nobody else does.

Officer Coleman says loudly, "Show us this room you spoke about."

I shiver inside. The punishment room.

I lead them up the stairs towards the place I fear the most. A room I never had access to unless I was dragged there in fear. Richard kept the key and was the only one who could open the door. I avoided it as much as I could but now it will be my salvation.

I see it at the end of the hallway and the shivers start. In a whisper, I say, "There it is."

DI Jones starts towards it and officer Coleman walks behind me, propelling me towards the place I fear the most.

I swallow hard as he opens the door and I briefly register it's unlocked before the door opens and we head inside.

I blink in disbelief as I look around the pretty room that looks welcoming and cosy. Pictures look down from the walls showing Richard and me at our happiest. They were taken at a time we were in love. In one I am laughing at something he says as he gazes at me with affection and in another, we share a kiss on a beach at sunset. The room itself is pretty and clean and is furnished beautifully with no sense of the horror it used to contain.

Officer Coleman says wearily, "Is this the room you spoke of?"

I shake my head wildly, "No… yes… but not this, it's different."

Officer Coleman says roughly, "So, you are saying you were tied to this bed and subjected to punishment against your will."

I look at the pretty bed that is made up of sumptuous bedding and an array of scatter cushions and even I can see there is no way a person could be tied to it. I say miserably, "It's different. This isn't the same room."

I can tell their patience is wearing thin and say with increasing urgency. "It's changed. He must have changed it. I'm telling you, there was nothing in here but a metal bed, a mattress and a bucket. The walls were painted dark, and the shutters boarded up the windows. I was tied to the metal bed and stripped naked sometimes for days. I'm telling you the truth."

I start to cry and hear the solicitor say angrily, "Enough. You have questioned my client for close on three days and now you have to decide to either charge her or release her. What's it to be officers?"

Officer Jones says with resignation. "We will head back to the station and work out where we go from here."

As I turn my back on the room that held so much pain, I hear him mocking me. Richard has made sure I will never be free. Wherever he is, he has planned this down to the finest detail. I am no match for him, that's obvious. Whatever happens next is out of my control because five years ago I gave that to him. I know it looks bad. I know I have nothing to back up my story and he appears to have his watertight. However, one thing he can't change is that I am free of him. I will never again have to fear his moods and subsequent punishment. Even if I go to prison, it will be preferable to a life with him.

As I walk away from the house we shared, I walk a little taller and with determination. He will not win and he will not break me. I will fight for my life because one thing's for sure, Richard will slip up and one day everyone will know what a monster he really is.

Chapter Twelve

I had crossed the line. I was free; but there was no one to welcome me to the land of freedom. I was a stranger in a strange land. Harriet Tubman

"I'm sorry, what?"

I feel my legs shake, as once again, I sit facing the two officers in the interview room with my solicitor by my side.

"We're releasing you."

I stare at them in surprise as officer Jones says roughly, "We have no body, so can't charge you with murder or manslaughter. You have however, been charged with causing death by dangerous driving in the case of Ellie Matthews and will be bound to appear in court at a later date. It's been decided that you'll remain under house arrest until the trial and so we are releasing you to return home as your bail has been set and paid for."

I stare at him in confusion. "Bail? Who paid it?"

He shrugs. "A Gloria Williams."

"Gloria? My neighbour Gloria?"

Officer Coleman nods. "Apparently, she believes your story and came forward with the money to set you free. Someone is on your side it seems."

I nod in disbelief because she was the last person I ever thought would step up to help me.

It doesn't take long until I am standing on the now familiar drive after the police gave me a ride home. Once again, I feel the silence surrounding me. Strangely there is no life left in the street. If my neighbours are home, you wouldn't know it.

As I stand in front of my house, I try to muster the courage to go inside. Officer Coleman has accompanied me and despite the situation, I feel comfortable with him around. Once again, number 15 Richmond Avenue, will be my prison, although this time it's different. This time it's a solitary one as the events of that night have created a different kind of future.

The man beside me says in a kind voice. "Will you be ok?"

I shake my head and say sadly, "No, I don't think I will be. This house holds many painful memories, and it's difficult to go inside."

I almost think he's going to take my hand and comfort me. I can't explain it but it's as if he… cares.

Then something enters my mind that I can't believe passed me by. The panic envelops me in a hold that chokes the words from my lips as I say with a fearful whisper, "What if Richard comes back?"

I look around, almost expecting to see him charging angrily towards me. Officer Coleman says gently, "Then you must call us immediately."

I begin to shake. How did I not consider this? He will come back. I know in my heart he will. I begin to shake and this time officer Coleman takes my arm in a reassuring act of kindness and says softly,

"If your husband returns it will be for the best. Everything will be explained and you will be free of that charge at least."

I stare at him with fear in my eyes and say fearfully, "I will never be free of him. He lives inside my head, my heart and my soul. He has damaged me beyond repair and I will spend the rest of my life waiting for him to return."

I take a step back and shake my head. "I'm sorry, I can't go in there, I can't do this. Please, take me back to the station, to prison, in fact, anywhere but here. I can't live here waiting for him to make his move, please don't make me, I'm begging you."

I can't control what's happening and start to sob as the fear visits me again and sets up home. I can't cope, it's too much and I break down on my driveway in front of the whole neighbourhood.

Suddenly, I hear footsteps racing towards me and feel a firm hand grasp my shoulder and pull me up. I hear a familiar voice say with a strength I could use right now, "It's ok, honey, I'm here for you. You're not on your own."

Through my tears I see Gloria looking at me with a fierce expression. She has a strength to her that rubs a little onto me as she says firmly, "Come, we'll go inside together. I won't leave you; I promise. You're safe with me, you know that, don't you?"

She places her arm around me and says to the officer angrily, "Well, don't just stand there, help me get her inside."

He moves to the other side of me and together we head inside the house that I hoped never to see again.

Gloria gasps as we stand looking at a space that is usually in order and so clean you could eat your dinner off the floor. Nothing has changed since the last time I stood here. The investigators have moved on, but they have left behind a crime scene.

Gloria says angrily, "What the hell is this? Couldn't you have cleared up or something? Poor Sarah, coming home to this."

The officer shrugs. "We are investigating a crime not running a maid service. This isn't our mess to clean."

Gloria shakes her head and looks around in disbelief but I just stare unseeing. I couldn't care less. The sight of Richard's blood on the walls reminds me he isn't here – yet at least. The sight of the upturned furniture and broken glass fills me happiness because I am used to seeing everything in its place which also means he isn't here. Richard couldn't bear to see this disorganised home which settles my heart. The house is the same but now very different. Maybe now, I get to live in a different way and that thought soothes my soul - a little.

The officer clears his throat and says gently, "I'll leave you to settle in."

His words bring my attention back to the situation and I say desperately, "Please can you just check that nobody's here before you go?"

I see them share a look and then he smiles gently. "Of course, I'll make sure it's secure."

As he heads off to search the house, Gloria shakes her head and says kindly, "I'll make you a cup of tea and then help you sort this mess out. Don't worry, honey, as I said, you're not on your own. I'll stay with you all the time you need me."

I stare at her with gratitude and say shakily, "Thank you, Gloria."

She smiles softly. "Don't thank me, it's the least I could do. I should have been here months ago. I should have listened to my inner voice that told me something was wrong and I should have been a better friend. Don't thank me, Sarah because I don't deserve your thanks. I knew something was wrong, I saw it in your eyes. On the surface you had it all but when you looked at me, I saw a different story playing out in your eyes. I chose to ignore it. It wasn't my problem and nothing to do with me. So, I carried on with life pushing it away until the next time I saw you and it all came flooding back. So many times, I wanted to ask you if anything was wrong and so many times, I told myself it was none of my business. Now I regret every moment when I wasn't the friend I should have been. Well, not anymore. I will stay by your side until the dust settles and you pull through. Because you will, honey. This is just a moment in time. A crazy situation that needs to play out before you can move on. And you will. It may take a while but one day you will look back and be grateful that this happened because you have been given a second shot at life. Now you must seize that opportunity with both hands and make it the best damned life you can. Take the lessons you have learned from this one and move forward with determination and courage. You're not alone in this, I'm with you every step of the way."

"Good advice."

My head spins as I see officer Coleman looking at us thoughtfully from the doorway. His eyes flick to Gloria and he says firmly, "Would you be willing to make a statement to that effect – you know, what you just said?"

She nods with a determination that settles my heart a little. "Of course, officer. I will do everything I can to help Sarah. It's a little late but I want to make things right."

He nods and then smiles gently. "Sarah. I have checked every room, cupboard and window. They are all secure and there is nobody else here. If you're worried, I can arrange for a panic alarm to be installed which will send a signal to the station if you trigger it."

I look at him gratefully and nod. "Please… that would help."

He nods. "I'll organise it. Now, I must be getting back."

He produces a card from his jacket pocket and places it beside the phone. "This is my direct line. Call me anytime night or day if you need me or remember anything. I will keep you informed of the case and if you have any questions, I'm happy to help. I understand you have Miss Wilson's number too."

I nod, remembering the kind words of the solicitor as she reassured me everything would be ok. The officer smiles and turns to Gloria, saying in a strangely gentle voice, "Look after her, Gloria. The same goes for you, call me anytime if you need to. I'll be in touch regarding your statement."

I watch them leave as Gloria shows him out and look around at the place I once called home. So much has changed since that night and only time will tell if it's for the better.

Chapter Thirteen

You gain strength, courage, and confidence by every experience in which you really stop to look fear in the face. You are able to say to yourself, 'I lived through this horror. I can take the next thing that comes along.' Eleanor Roosevelt

We work hard trying to restore order to a place that will never be the same again. As we work, I talk and tell Gloria everything. I start at the beginning and she stays silent as I offload what I should have done years ago. I can tell she pities me but I can't help that. *I* pity me because I wasn't strong enough to stand up to a bully. Gloria, as it turns out, is a rock in my hour of need.

She stays with me and we even order take out. Not that I have much of an appetite but I humour her and work my way through the Chinese meal she ordered and try to make sense of the situation.

Even that first night she stays. Gloria doesn't leave my side for a minute and there are no words to express how grateful I am.

The first night back at number 15 is a fitful one. I can't sleep expecting Richard to walk through the door at any moment. As I lie in our bed, the memories flood my mind for most of the night. Gloria stays in the spare room and I leave my door open in case I need to call out. I feel secure knowing she's here but I still live with the fear. He will be back; I just know it.

The second night is much the same with a slight difference. This time I sleep fitfully and the nightmares start. This time Gloria sits beside me as I scream with fear. This time she holds me as I sob on her shoulder and this time the nightmares are more intense and believable.

The third night, I think I hear someone trying to get in and scream the house down. Gloria takes charge and makes certain the house is locked and secure and promises me no harm will come to me.

The fourth night *she* comes.

The girl on Gander Green lane. Ellie Matthews. The one innocent person in all of this and the person with the kindest eyes I have ever seen. She sits beside me in my bed and comforts me. She doesn't speak but the look in her eyes says it all. It's that same serene look that promises things will get better. It's the look of understanding and one of hope. It's the look of a friendship that has developed with no words spoken and it's the look of forgiveness.

This girl doesn't hate me as I deserve. She is comforting me and telling me she's happy. We have never spoken yet she knows everything about me. It's in that look and with her beside me, I can do anything. She is my strength, my heartbeat and my soul. I always wished I was that girl; she is giving me the strength to be that girl in the future.

On the fifth night, Gloria returns home and it begins.

Despite everything, I have settled into a routine. I am still trying to come to terms with it all but somehow, life is working its way into something that almost passes for normal. I get up, wash, dress and try to occupy my time. I sort through drawers, cupboards, anything to take my mind off my situation.

Gloria left with the promise to check on me regularly. She had to return home because she does have a life outside of this nightmare.

She is the only one who visits. No other neighbours knock on the door with kind words or offerings of support. The only time the phone rings is when officer Coleman or Miss Williams call to update me on the case. I watch the television with half an ear because I am not interested in anything it has to say. I just need to hear voices and bring some life into a dead space.

I don't need to worry about work because I am now officially redundant. There is enough money and the bills are all being paid automatically and I have everything I need – except my freedom. I've been told to stay inside - not venture out and call if I need anything. If I run, Gloria will lose her bail money and I would never do that to her. I'm a prisoner in my own home which is nothing I haven't been before.

Tonight, is my first night alone and I approach it with trepidation. I fill the house with voices from the television but know they will soon be silenced when I sleep.

As usual, I wash and get ready for bed and make myself a warm drink to try to help me sleep. I make sure the house is secure and leave a light on downstairs and one on the landing. I can't sleep without it because the shadows bring the monsters inside.

As I climb into bed, I turn my back on the side Richard used to occupy. It feels strange sleeping here but I need to do this. I need to face every challenge this situation is throwing at me and make myself carry on as I'd have done before this all happened. If I sleep in the guest room, he's won.

For the first time since I returned home there are no nightmares. I fall to sleep relatively quickly and there are no bad dreams to wake me in fear.

Then I hear it.

It starts off quietly and seeps into my unconscious before bringing me to reality. The haunting, classical musical that Richard loved so much. The same tune that played in the car on the night of the accident starts to play through the house, waking me and sending terror to my heart.

I sit bolt upright and start shaking as the haunting melody weaves a tangled web of fear around my heart. The volume increases and fills my ears causing them to hurt. I scream but it can't be heard above the noise and my sobs are carried away by the music as it reminds me I will never be free.

On shaking legs, I stand and go in search of the source. Grabbing a flashlight from the bedside table, I move fearfully toward the hallway. The weight of the flashlight sits reassuringly in my hand because it serves as a weapon if needed. All the time the music plays, causing the memory of that night to resurface in all its horror and I feel my heart thumping wildly with every step I take.

The phone is downstairs and I berate myself for not keeping it with me at all times. The panic button is situated in the hall but it seems as if I must cross a continent to reach it.

The terror accompanies me on my voyage of discovery. My heart beats a steady rhythm to the sound of the music and I think I hold my breath with every step I take. All the time I fully expect to see him. Richard, the man who told me I would pay.

Edging toward the stairs, I look around fearfully. The music is melancholy and weaves a spell of fear around my heart. I swallow hard as I strain to hear any other sound than the hateful music that reminds me of that night and *him*.

With every step I take, I fully expect to see him. How did he get in? I have bolted all the doors and windows. Surely, if he had a key, it would be rendered useless against the bolts inside.

Then the fear grips me. What if he was inside all along? Did the officer search every nook and cranny? Did he check the loft space and what if

Richard snuck in during the day in an unguarded moment? I know he's here because who else would know? Who else would set that music playing, knowing how symbolic that tune is?

As my bare feet hit the carpet of the bottom step, I see the panic button before me like a welcome friend. I don't stop to think in my need for help. Rushing across the hall, I hammer my fist down onto it and pray it works. Then, I grab the phone and with shaking fingers, dial the number programmed in the phone for officer Coleman.

Chapter Fourteen

I am not afraid of an army of lions led by a sheep; I am afraid of an army of sheep led by a lion.
Alexander the Great

All the time the music plays until I don't think it can get any louder. I daren't venture into the room it plays from. What if he's waiting?

Then he answers, sleepy and distant. "Officer Coleman."

The music stops.

I say with fear in my voice. "Please, can you come? It's Sarah Standon. I think someone's in the house."

Instantly, his voice is more alert, and he says quickly, "Have you pushed the panic alarm?"

I whisper, "Yes."

"Good, the police are on their way. I'll be over as quickly as I can. As soon as they arrive, let them in, until then, stay on the phone."

I nod, thinking he can see me and he says sharply, "Did you hear me, Sarah?"

I whisper, "Yes… please hurry."

He says softly, "Don't worry, help is coming. Where are you now?"

"I'm in the hallway. I think someone's here. There was music… loud music. The same music *he* played."

"Is the music still playing, Sarah?"

I whisper, "No."

Before he can reply, I hear a sharp knock on the door which makes me jump, and he says, "Was that a knock?"

"Yes."

I see the blue flash of the sirens reflected in the window and my heart sinks with relief.

Officer Coleman says sharply, "Open the door and let the officers search the house."

I stand and creep towards the door and say in a frightened whisper, "What if it's him?"

He says wearily, "Check the window. If you see a police car, it's them."

Doing as he says; I check the window and see two police officers and a dog outside and my heart settles. I'm safe.

I say gratefully, "They're here. I'm opening the door."

He says briskly, "I'm going to hang up now but I'll be right over."

As I cut the call, I open the door and the officers look at me with serious expressions. "Is everything ok, Ma'am?"

I say shakily, "I think somebody was in here."

They share a look and one of the officers takes my arm and says kindly, "Stay with me while they search the place. If anyone's here, we'll soon know about it."

I watch as the other officer unleashes the dog and follows him from room to room. The dog is magnificent to watch as they sweep the place in what appears to be seconds. The other officer turns on the lights and takes me to sit on the couch while we wait. When the others return, we hear, "All clear, there's nothing."

My shoulders sag with relief and as the officer and his dog leave, the other says kindly, "What did you hear?"

I shake my head. "Music. I woke up to loud, classical music. It was the same music my husband played and the song he played on the night of the accident. It was deafening me and yet when I called officer Coleman, it stopped."

The look the officer gives me tells me he thinks I'm crazy. Maybe I am but I know what I heard.

We sit in an awkward silence for a few minutes until officer Coleman appears. He nods to the other officer and says sharply, "What did you find?"

Shaking his head, he says wearily, "Nothing."

Officer Coleman looks at me and says gently, "You did the right thing, Sarah. Let me make you a cup of tea and you can tell me what happened."

He nods to the other officer. "It's fine, I've got this. Thanks, Pete."

The officer smiles sympathetically and says brightly, "Take care, Sarah. We're always here if you need us, don't hesitate to call if you need help."

I smile at him gratefully. "Thank you for coming. I'm sorry to waste your time."

He smiles. "You didn't. We're on duty, so it's all in a night's work to us. Take care of yourself."

He leaves and I watch officer Coleman busy himself with making the tea and feel bad. I say sadly, "I'm sorry… um… officer Coleman."

He sets the mug before me and says lightly, "Call me Tony. Officer Coleman is a bit of a mouthful."

I smile, taking a sip of the tea gratefully. "Then thank you, Tony. If I'm honest, I feel a little foolish now."

He sits opposite me at the table and smiles kindly. "Tell me what happened."

I laugh a little self-consciously. "I woke up to the sound of music – classical music. The same song that was playing the night of the crash. It started off quietly and then became so loud it drowned out my screams. I was so frightened, I thought Richard was here."

He looks around and says firmly, "Where is your music system?"

I point towards the study and say shakily, "In Richard's office."

He nods and says firmly, "Show me."

Taking a deep breath, I stand to follow him. I lead him to Richard's study and open the door, almost expecting to see him sitting behind the desk. It's not a room I ever enter unless it's to clean. This is Richard's space and one I'm unwelcome in. It's surrounded by wood panelling and smells of the usual sandalwood polish he loves. As expected, everything is in its proper place and I hover in the doorway as Tony heads inside.

I watch him move across to the desk, behind which sits the music system. I hold my breath as he presses a button, and the music fills the room. However, this is not the music I heard. This is a different sound altogether. It's an album of easy listening jazz tracks that's nothing like what I just heard.

Tony says, "Is this the music?"

I shake my head. "No."

He presses another button and the sound of the radio fills the air. This time it's a programme that plays no music. A station that has conversation rather than music and my heart sinks as I see the doubt enter Tony's eyes. He fiddles with it some more but nothing comes close to what I heard. He shrugs and smiles sympathetically. "Maybe it was the radio after all. You never know what they play at night. Perhaps something triggered the system to come on, or maybe you were dreaming which sometimes explains things that happen at night."

I shake my head angrily. "I wasn't dreaming. I would know. It stopped the second you answered the phone. How was that me dreaming?"

He smiles sympathetically. "I don't know but whatever it was, it's gone now. If it makes you feel any better, I'll unplug the system and then it won't happen again. Is this the only one in the house?"

I nod miserably. "Yes."

Just for a second, he stares and then shakes his head, saying kindly. "Listen, you've been through a traumatic experience. You took a blow to the head and your husband is missing. Things are bound to be a little crazy while the dust settles. Maybe you should get checked out by the doctor. Just to be on the safe side."

His words, although meant to be kind, sting a little as I can tell he doesn't believe me. However, even I know he's probably right. Maybe it was my mind playing a cruel trick on me. Is it possible to sleepwalk and your dream mirror reality? I know it probably is, so I smile sadly and say with a little embarrassment, "I'm sorry... Tony. You must think I'm a crazy woman."

He smiles which makes him seem a lot more human and grins. "We're all a little crazy from time to time. I think you're allowed to be after what happened to you. I'm serious about the doctor though. You should get checked out; you may have something they overlooked."

He looks around and says brightly, "I'll just check everything's secure and there's nobody hiding under your bed or in the cupboard."

He grins taking the sting from his words and I relax slightly. "Then I'll leave you to get some sleep."

He hesitates in the doorway and then turns back and says gently, "Do you have any family you can call?"

I shake my head ruefully. "None that would welcome it."

He moves across and sits down beside me and says softly, "Why, what happened?"

My eyes fill with tears as I think about my parents. Two kind, generous souls who didn't deserve the daughter fate dealt them.

I say miserably, "Richard didn't like them."

Tony raises his eyes and I look at him in shame. "When I met Richard, I was so happy. I introduced him to my parents after we had been going steady for a few weeks. I'm not sure why but my father took an instant dislike to him. My mother was a little more diplomatic but I could tell by the expression in her eyes she shared my father's view. I couldn't understand it. What wasn't to like? He was good looking, charming and successful. He treated me like a princess and was kind and loving to everyone he met. But they hated him on sight. Richard obviously picked up on it and it caused many arguments. I was besotted with him and so started to distance myself from them. When Richard asked me to marry him, we sought their approval. You know, the old-fashioned way."

Tony smiles and I shrug ruefully. "They told us they couldn't give us their blessing. Well, you can imagine how that went down. I was angry and so was Richard but they stood firm. My father wouldn't give me away and they wanted no part in the wedding."

Tony says in a shocked voice. "That must have hurt – a lot."

I nod sadly. "It did. I pleaded, begged and cajoled them but they wouldn't budge. In the end, we moved away, and I had nothing more to do with them. Richard told me all the time we were married I wasn't to have any contact with them. He wiped them from our lives and they don't even know where we live."

Tony looks shocked and I feel ashamed of myself. I smile through my tears. "I regret every harsh word spoken and above all, that I didn't listen. I should have seen what was obvious to them. Richard wasn't the man for me, he was the monster under my bed and the man I should have avoided at all costs. Even now, I can't bring myself to call which shows you just how low I've sunk. What daughter turns her back on her parents and doesn't even know if they're still alive? I'm ashamed of myself, Tony and don't deserve their sympathy now."

To his credit, Tony doesn't react. He remains impassive and just smiles gently and says softly, "You should call them. You may be surprised by what you find."

He stands to leave and I say, "Thank you. I mean that, you've been amazing."

He shakes his head. "Just doing my job, Sarah. You may not be so happy to see me next time I call."

His words remind me I'm still under investigation and am, in fact, a criminal in his eyes. He looks around and says firmly. "Bolt the door after me and try to get some sleep. I've checked everywhere and you're perfectly safe."

I follow him to the door and do as he says. As I hear his steps move away, it enhances the loneliness I feel. Maybe I should reach out to my parents – maybe something good could come out of this after all.

Chapter Fifteen

Someday everything will make perfect sense. So for now, laugh at the confusion, smile through the tears and keep reminding yourself that everything happens for a reason. – unknown

I sleep in for the first time in years. The sun is high in the sky when I drag myself downstairs to get some coffee and for a while, everything seems normal.

I take my mug over to the window and watch the world going about its day. Mrs Barlow is cleaning her windows. I see Angela walk to her car and wonder how she's feeling now she's pregnant. I see Carrie Evans lifting a child into her car as she heads out on the school run and then I see her husband Derek kiss her on the cheek affectionately as he heads off to the office.

Normal life goes on for everyone but me, Richard and the girl on Gander Green lane. We are altered forever. One is dead, killed in her prime and will always be remembered with love and fondness. One is on the run and sure to return and cause more trouble, and one may as well be dead, although some may argue she has been for years. One person is a prisoner of her own stupidity and only has herself to blame for the situation she finds herself in.

Sighing, I head off to get dressed and tackle yet another cupboard in a bid to distract my attention. It must be around 10 o clock when Gloria knocks on the door.

"Hey, Sarah. It's only me, I've come bearing gifts."

Grateful for some company, I fling open the door and smile as Gloria heads inside, staggering under the weight of some shopping bags.

"Phew, they're heavier than I thought."

I look with interest as she starts pulling all sorts of treasures from them. Beautiful clothing that looks almost new, sits alongside fabulous handbags and designer scarves. I look at her in surprise and she says warmly, "I thought you could use a change of clothes. You must be craving something new and I thought some of these would help banish those unhappy memories."

I'm actually speechless as I look at her with gratitude. "How did you know?"

She smiles sadly. "I'm guessing every item you own brings back unhappy memories. I know I'm the same. I remember things that happen by the clothes I wear. For instance, I had a puncture not so long ago and had to wait for hours in the pouring rain. The dress I was wearing got soaked through and I haven't worn it since – bad luck you see. Then there's the skirt I wore when I got my latest health check. It didn't go well so obviously the skirt is bad luck and I dropped it to the charity shop."

I look at her with concern. "Are you ok, health wise I mean?"

She shrugs. "So, so. I had a negative smear test and had to get some treatment. It seems ok now, but I was worried for a while there."

I smile sadly, "I'm sorry, I never knew."

Gloria smiles ruefully. "There are a lot of things we never knew about each other. I suppose I always knew something was wrong in your life, Sarah. This perfect life you had going should have told me it was a lie. I mean, nobody lives like you did. The house and garden were always immaculate. Your husband appeared to have been made in a factory for designer husbands. Yet, somehow your eyes were sad. Tortured in fact and I never asked. I shrugged it off and went about my business wishing my life was as charmed as yours."

I look at her in surprise. "Are you saying you're unhappy?"

"Aren't we all? Nothing is perfect. There's never enough money and we scrape by as best we can. My husband is irritable most of the time and I can't remember the last time we had a meaningful conversation. The only child I have lives with her father and his new wife and the dog died last month."

She wipes a tear from her eye as I stare at her feeling bad. I remember when her dog died. One minute he was there, the next I heard he had an illness and was put to sleep. I never once went to see her. I didn't think to take her a plant or chocolates to cheer her up. I never thought to offer a listening ear while she grieved because like she said, it was easier to pretend it wasn't happening. Easier to smile and close the door on another's problems. I had more than my fair share of my own but that's no excuse. I wasn't there for her like she is for me.

I say with interest, "Do you think everyone's the same? I mean, look around us. We live in a respectable neighbourhood where everyone appears happy and to have life worked out. Do you think their lives are filled with problems and secrets like mine?"

Gloria smiles wickedly, "Of course, they have secrets. However, some are not so secretive, if you know what I mean."

She pulls out the chair and reaches for a bottle of wine. "Sit yourself down, Sarah and prepare to be amazed."

I don't even register that it's still morning as Gloria fills two glasses with wine and smiles. "Ok, take Angela for instance."

"What, pregnant Angela?"

She nods and lowers her voice, even though we are the only ones here. "I heard she couldn't get pregnant for a reason."

I shake my head and she says, "Her husband. They've been trying for ages and no luck. I know because she asked me ages ago if I knew anywhere they could go to for advice. Well, she went alright and apparently got a lot more than the advice she was seeking."

"What do you mean?"

"The 'advisor' turned out to be a flame from the past which was quickly re-kindled on the office floor. Then wham, bam pregnant mam."

I stare at her in shock and she shakes her head. "I only know because my friend Joanne works in the same office and saw Angela hurrying from the scene rearranging her clothing. Apparently, this guy is well known for charming the ladies and is under investigation as we speak."

"But you don't know the baby's his?"

Gloria shrugs. "Maybe, maybe not but rather a coincidence wouldn't you say? The truth, however, will be in the end result. If that baby looks like her advisor the shit will hit the fan."

"Why, does Vincent suspect?"

She shrugs. "Who knows but I'm guessing our friend Angela is a bundle of nerves and hormones right now."

I take a swig of the wine and she carries on. "You know Sally and Crispin."

I nod, fascinated by what she's saying. "Well, apparently they're swingers."

I almost spit my wine across the table. "Swingers!"

She laughs loudly. "You know that retreat they go to every year in Sweden. Swingersville."

I start to giggle as she carries on. "I saw the name of the place they were going and googled it.

I'm not lying when I say that place should be on the dark web. Even the website was X rated. Come to think of it, I may have seen a picture of Sally and Crispin in the background on one of the promotional shots."

Laughing, I shake my head. "Now you're making it up."

She shrugs. "Maybe but I know what I saw. You know, Edward always said there was something fishy about that couple and now I know what he meant."

My sides are aching from laughing and I gasp, "Stop, you're so wicked."

She giggles and takes another swig of wine. "That's not all. Did you know they ordered a new hot tub? Well, I'm not accepting any invitations to try that out in the near future. They are probably looking for like-minded individuals to share their... um... hobby."

As we giggle like schoolgirls, I forget for a minute. Just for a moment, I am normal. A carefree woman having fun with a friend. This is what it should be like. Not living in fear 24/7 and worried about absolutely everything.

She must notice the change in my expression because she smiles gently, "Are you ok, honey?"

I sigh heavily. "I was just thinking how much fun this is. It's made me realise what I've missed out on all these years. My whole life revolved around Richard and what he wanted. I never once thought about me and what I needed. Maybe if I had, I would have spoken up sooner. Made a stand and not let myself fall down the rabbit hole with him."

Reaching out, Gloria takes my hand and smiles sympathetically. "We're all guilty of that, honey. So wrapped up in the here and now we don't step back to see the bigger picture. I'm guessing you just wanted to make your husband happy in the early days. You fell in love and wanted to hold on to that feeling for as long as possible. Maybe when it went, you thought you could get it back if you just toed the line and did what made him happy. It's perfectly understandable but just remember one thing, he took more than he should. He ruined you, honey and you can't blame yourself for that. What happened was always going to happen. Two weeks from now or two years, something was always going to make you snap, or worse. It could be you lying in that mortuary instead. Just remember everything happens for a reason and it may not be clear now but the whole picture will reveal itself in time."

Gloria smiles and looks at her watch. "Talking of time, I must fly. My personal trainer is due in two hours and I need to prepare."

I raise my eyes, "Prepare?"

She winks, "Put it this way, it's the *personal* bit of trainer I look forward to the most."

Shaking my head, I say quickly, "I thought you were struggling to make ends meet."

She laughs. "I'd give up food if it meant I kept Byron. Some things are necessities, darling. The luxuries like meals out with the husband are a sacrifice I'm willing to make."

She winks as she grabs her purse and keys and heads to the door. "Enjoy trying on the clothes. I'm going to enjoy taking mine off."

As she heads home, she leaves a smile on my face. Gloria is just what I needed today. A real tonic and once again, I wish I had known how great she was before. Maybe, just maybe, things would have turned out differently.

Chapter Sixteen

We don't develop courage by being happy every day. We develop it by surviving difficult times and challenging adversity. Barbara De Angelis

Three days later and I'm going stir crazy. I haven't seen a soul since Gloria left and I think I've cleared out every cupboard in the house. So, when the doorbell rings, I almost run to answer it. Even if it's somebody selling their religion, I'll ask them in, I am so starved of conversation I've resorted to talking to myself.

However, as soon as I wrench the door open, I wish I hadn't because glaring at me through hate-filled eyes is Sylvia, Richard's mother.

I take a step back as she pushes her way in and snarls, "You bitch."

"Excuse me."

The fury in her eyes makes me stop in my tracks as she shouts angrily, "What have you done? You stupid, stupid bitch. My son is missing because of you and I want to know where he is. What have you done to him?"

I take a step back as she advances slowly. I see the madness in her eyes as she pushes me into a corner and I stutter, "I ... I... I... don't know. He ran away from the scene of the accident. I don't know where he is."

Slap.

The blow to my face causes my head to snap back and I feel my face smarting from the power behind it.

"Liar. You've killed him, haven't you? You murdered my son and now expect us to live with the uncertainty. You can't even let a mother grieve for her son because you won't tell us where you've hidden the body. Well, I'm here to beat it out of you. You'll wish you had died that night when I've finished with you."

She raises her hand again and I start to scream. "Get out. You have no right to be here. Get out!"

I watch in disbelief as the tears run like rapids down her cheeks as she cries like a mad woman, "Tell me, tell me where you've hidden his body."

I shake my head as Tony rushes through the door and steps between us. He says firmly, "Enough, Mrs Standon. Leave Sarah alone, you are not supposed to be here."

My knees tremble with the shock as he pushes her gently back and then she wails so loudly I think the whole neighbourhood must hear her. "I want my son. I want him back with me where he belongs. Make her speak because god knows I will if you don't."

I watch as Tony frogmarches Sylvia out of the house and sit shaking on the ground. I can't believe what just happened. She was so broken. Despite my hatred of her, I felt compassion towards her. She was devastated and like me, must be wondering where on earth he is? How could he do this to her –

his own mother? Why wouldn't he let her know he was safe, why is he doing this to us?

I am still in the same crouched position when Tony returns. Gently, he takes my hand and pulls me up and leads me over to the couch. He says softly, "Are you ok?"

I shake my head sadly, "Not really, Tony. Do you think there'll come a time when I ever will be again?"

He nods. "You will be. I've been in this job long enough to know that even when things are at their worst there is always that spark of hope that lights the way out. You will get through this. Whatever happens, life will go on and you will pick yours up and move forward."

I whisper, "How is that possible when Richard is still out there? What if he comes back, he would kill me, I just know it?"

I start to shiver at the thought and Tony wraps a nearby blanket around my shoulders. "You're in shock, you need to take some deep breaths and let your body process what just happened. One step at a time, that's all you need to take."

I'm not sure why but his words strike something deep inside me that yearns for a friendly word and loving smile. It yearns for that security that only a loved one can give you and it yearns for this nightmare to be over. At this moment, I feel more alone than I have ever been. Even lonelier than when I used to lie in the punishment room. I am on my own – period. I may have two kind people looking out for me but when the door closes at night, it's just me and my nightmares.

I must say this out loud because Tony looks worried as I say softly, "There's no way out… for me, anyway."

Strangely he puts an arm around my shoulder and hugs me reassuringly. His voice is soft and gentle as he whispers, "You will pull through this. You're a fighter and this is a fight worth winning. Don't give in because you have so much to live for. This mess will sort itself out but it will take time. But time passes and you will come out the other side. Stay strong, Sarah and show everyone how invincible you really are."

Smiling through my tears, I nod and whisper, "Thanks, Tony."

Just for a second, he says and does nothing. We sit together like old friends that may wish to share something a little more. It feels nice, comforting and natural. Is this feeling wrong – probably but I'm past caring? I need a Tony in my life now more than ever because loneliness is a terrible feeling and reminds me how weak I am. Even now, I am leaning on a man to get me through life. I need to shape up because if I don't sort my head out, I may as well have died that night because this life I'm living isn't worth fighting for.

Tony stayed with me for a while and when he left, the thought didn't even cross my mind as to why he was here in the first place.

Chapter Seventeen

Being alone with fear can rapidly turn into panic.
Being alone with frustration can rapidly turn into
anger. Being alone with disappointment can rapid
turn into discouragement and, even worse, despair.
Mark Goulston

That night I'm woken by a baby crying.

My eyes snap open and I make out the distinctive cry of a newborn baby coming from somewhere in the house. My heart starts hammering and I feel a nervous sweat break out across my whole body. What is that?

My legs shake as I try to stand. It's like the music all over again. Is this another trick? Another recording designed to instil fear because if so, it's working.

My teeth chatter as I put one foot in front of the other as I grab the flashlight. This time the phone is beside my bed but I'm too scared to call Tony. If I press the panic alarm, I know it will stop and the police will have me labelled as a crazy woman who is turning slightly psychotic. No, I need to be brave and deal with this on my own and put a stop to this one way or another.

The sound fills my head as the baby screams as if in pain. The sobs push their way from inside me as I stumble in the darkness. I snap on the bedroom light hoping it will make everything go away.

Darkness has a habit of making the normal appear dangerous. It disguises everyday objects making them appear sinister and if I thought that one simple act would chase the shadows away; I was wrong.

It gets louder.

My heart thumps with every step I take as I head towards the sound. Is this real, am I imagining this because I must be? Surely.

I checked every door, every window and every room bar one before I went to sleep. It's that room that stands at the end of the hall taunting me and promising to punish me for daring to think I will ever be free. That room is the root of all evil and stands as a symbol of my own weakness. That room is where the baby is crying.

Something snaps inside me. I turn towards the punishment room and the anger flares up inside me as I storm towards it. Enough. I will not live in fear anymore. If Richard is there, he can kill me because this isn't living, anyway. I want to end this once and for all and only I can do that.

I start to talk over the noise just trying to drown out the desperate cries. Anything to drive the fear away because it is choking me as I walk. Squeezing all rational thought from my brain as I head to the room that I hate the most.

The noise intensifies along with the fear. My heart beats so fast I may not have long to live but I need to see. I need to face whatever this is because how can I ever move on unless I do?

With one hand on the door handle, I hesitate for the briefest second before taking a deep breath and then I open the door, quickly, fiercely and with determination and shout loudly, "I know it's you, Richard. I'm not afraid of you anymore, do you hear me?"

Then I scream.

I don't stop, I can't stop.

I stand in the doorway of the punishment room and the horror hits me hard. The punishment room is back in all its glory. The pretty room has gone. The walls are dark and the windows black. The metal bed stands alone in the middle of the room with the bucket by its side. This time, however, something is beside it. A baby's crib rocking wildly from side to side as a baby cries, desperately, painfully and agonising. I'm not sure where the baby's screams end and mine begin because I can't do anything else. I stand screaming as the full horror hits me. He's here.

I must have blacked out because when I come round, I'm lying on the rug on the floor of the punishment room. Except, once again, it's the pretty room. The walls are white and the furnishings cosy and pretty. The crib is gone and the photos stare down at me with sympathy and compassion.

I sit up and look around in disbelief. How can this be? I saw it, it was real – wasn't it? Am I going mad? I think I must be because how could this have changed so quickly? I rub my head and the pain reminds me I have an injury. It's easy to forget sometimes with all the madness surrounding my life but maybe that's the problem. I had a blow to the head, and it's messing with my mind.

I drag myself up from the floor and sit on the edge of the bed. I look at the canvas of Richard and me in happier times and remember where it was taken. We hadn't long been married. He surprised me with a trip to the coast for the weekend. He was always doing things like that. He was kind, attentive and loving and nothing like the monster he became. I smile as I remember how happy I was. We stayed in a cabin set among the sand dunes and it was magical. Nothing to do but each other and I thought life couldn't get any better. I was right. It never did.

As I look at the picture, I feel a sense of incredible sadness. We could have had so much. I'm not sure why things deteriorated so quickly but it didn't take long. We had only been married for one year before the cracks started to show.

Richard became more wrapped up in business. His patience was thin and things began to irritate him. I put it down to his stressful workload but it was something else. He was preoccupied and short with me. Where before he was kind and loving, now he was cruel and dismissive. Sex became harder, more brutal and at first, it excited me. I'm ashamed to admit I loved the passion involved. Then that was all that was left. Brutal sex and words of reassurance afterwards. Richard led me to believe it was in my best interests. He was doing this for my own good and I should thank him for it. I push the memory away of that first time. I'm not ready to deal with that yet. It's a memory I don't want to remember because I should have known then. I should have listened to the warning signs, but he convinced me otherwise.

Wearily, I drag myself from the bed and head towards my bedroom. I need to shower, change and then I will look for answers. I will take charge of my life and know just the place to start.

It feels forbidden and I should turn away but something is compelling me to dig. It feels wrong to sit behind his desk. It feels forbidden to open the drawers and rifle through them, almost like a thief in the night. I half expect him to come rushing in, shouting and berating me for daring to invade his personal space. But he doesn't and soon I am so engrossed in my task I lose all sense of time.

Like the man himself, Richard's desk is flawless. Everything in its place, neat and tidy, filed correctly and labelled methodically. Mostly it's household bills and work documents. I find nothing of interest which doesn't surprise me. I'm not sure what I thought I'd find, anyway.

Wearily, I keep on looking and discover the paperwork concerning the house. It all looks so boring and I flick through the contents with half a mind on something else. Then I come to the deeds of the house and it takes a while to register but then it hits me. The house is in my name only. This can't be right. I remember signing the deeds and even had a witness signature. Quickly, I look closer and read it through properly. The date is the same, just before the house became ours. Flicking through the paperwork, I see no trace of his name anywhere. This must be wrong. Surely.

For the next hour, I study every document in fine detail but his name is nowhere. It's as if he doesn't exist. I turn my attention to another file. The household bills. Once again, nothing to indicate he even lives here. Everything is in my name, even the one detailing the voting register. That can't be right. He voted I remember him doing it several times in fact. Why is he not listed under this address?

It's as if he doesn't exist - has never existed. Sinking back against the chair, I look into space trying hard to register what this means.

The sound of the phone ringing interrupts my thought process and I reach out and say breathlessly, "Sarah Standon."

There is nothing on the other end.

"Hello, can you hear me?"

Again, nothing and I make to cut the call when I hear a low whisper, "I told you I'd make you pay."

The fear grips my heart and twists it hard. Richard.

My legs start shaking as he says softly, "I am going to make you pay for the rest of your miserable life. You will never escape me, Sarah. This is the calm before the storm because I haven't even got started yet."

I say shakily, "Where are you?"

He laughs dully. "I am in your head, your heart and your world. You will never be free of me and the only time you will be is if I decide to let you go. But I never will, Sarah because you're mine. Always were, always will be, MINE! You thought you could escape, but you were wrong. I will always own you and you will soon discover what that means."

He slams the phone down and I drop mine as if it burns. Where is he?

My heart beats furiously as I grab hold of the phone and dial the number to reveal the last caller. There is nothing. No caller ID and I panic.

Richard is out there, stalking me and biding his time. Quickly, I dial Tony's number and he answers almost immediately, "Hey, Sarah, what's up?"

I say breathlessly, "Richard just called, please hurry."

He says firmly and with an authority I need right now. "Stay where you are, I'm on my way."

It only takes about twenty minutes before I hear the car pull up outside. I look out of the window and see his silver Volvo next to mine and almost run to the door. Wrenching it open, the words come thick and fast. "He called me - Richard. He told me he would make me pay. He's somewhere nearby, Tony. I know it's him. He's messing with my mind and torturing me at night. He wants to send me mad but I won't let him."

Tony reaches out and grabs hold of my arms. "Take a deep breath, Sarah. That's it, in and out, try to calm down and then you can tell me everything."

He helps me inside and sits beside me on the couch while I tell him what happened last night and then this morning. He looks at me thoughtfully. "That's all a bit weird. You say, there's no trace of his name on any paperwork."

I nod, my eyes filling with tears. "How is that possible?"

He shakes his head. "I'm not sure but I can look into it. There will be documented proof on the system somewhere that you both own this house if it was ever filed."

"What do mean, if?"

He looks at me kindly. "I'm sorry, Sarah but Richard was/is a solicitor. He will know every trick in the book to tie things up legally. It appears he's made it so you have everything. It may take a while but I'll box up the paperwork and get a team working on it. If he has done anything illegal, we will soon know about it."

I nod and then remember the call. "But he called me, Tony. I spoke to him and he was cold and threatening. He told me I would pay and I'd never be rid of him."

Tony jumps up and says firmly, "Which phone did you use?"

I lead him into Richard's office and point to the phone. "There. That one."

I watch as he dials the recall number but as I found out – nothing. Shrugging, he replaces it, saying, "I'll get on to the phone company. It won't be difficult to get a list of numbers who called here. Even if it's withheld, it will still be traceable."

He smiles kindly. "Listen, don't worry. You'll be fine. If Richard is out there, it's a good thing. It means he's alive. If he's alive, there is no crime to charge you with. Any little thing you can think of please tell me because it will work in your favour in the end. Every time he contacts you write it down and call me immediately. Like I said, if he is out there, we'll find him."

He turns to leave and I say falteringly, "Tony, what's happening with Ellie Matthews, you know, the girl on Gander Green lane?"

He looks at me sympathetically. "Her family are arranging the funeral. The body has been released to them as the investigation is over."

I think I hold my breath as I have to ask. "Where does that leave me?"

He crosses the room and pulls me down beside him and looks at me kindly. "I'm sorry, Sarah. Your solicitor will be in touch. Like I said, you were charged with causing death by dangerous driving. I know you said you weren't driving but we have two witnesses who will swear that you were. The case will go to court and you will be tried, and I expect convicted. It's likely to incur a prison term but I'm not sure how long that will be. Your only hope is that we find your husband, although even if we do, the evidence is pointing against you."

I feel the ever-present tears burning behind my eyes as I say fearfully, "But I wasn't driving. Richard was injured, his blood would be on the driver's seat, surely. Who are these witnesses who say they saw me because they're mistaken?"

He shakes his head and says firmly, "I can't tell you who they are but I can tell you the only blood we found of Richard's was on you. Your fingerprints are on the steering wheel and your DNA on the driver's seat. We did find Richards but that would be expected as he is your husband and would have had access to your car. However, there was no blood on the passenger seat and yours was on the steering wheel. This indicates that when your head hit the windscreen, it splashed onto it. I'm sorry, Sarah but nothing at all points to the fact that Richard was driving, only what you say. It doesn't look good I'm afraid."

I start to cry and he places his arm around my shoulders and says softly, "I'm sorry, I wish I had better news. The trouble is, the law deals with the facts and they don't lie. You need to prepare yourself for this because I'm guessing when the trial date is set, you will not like how it ends. Remember though, I am always here to help. I may be the officer on the case but I want to make it easier for you. This job, it's complicated. Feelings do get involved sometimes and yet I must remember I'm here to do a job. I wish things were different but I can't control that."

He stands and says sadly, "I should go. You need to think about what I said and maybe call your solicitor who can reassure you more than I can. Call your friend, in fact, call anyone you can because you shouldn't be alone right now. However, I'm not the best person to keep you company because ultimately, I am the one who will send you to prison."

He heads towards the door and I say through my tears, "Thank you."

He sighs heavily. "Don't thank me, Sarah, because right now I feel like a complete and utter bastard. I can tell you're a good woman. I can see you have struggled with something I don't fully understand but what I think doesn't matter. I wish things were different but they aren't. Maybe I should let officer Jones deal with this case because I'm getting too involved and it will only end badly."

I look at him in shock as he looks at me almost desperately. "I should go."

Standing up, I walk towards him slowly and a little unsure about what I'm going to do next. He falters a little as I reach him and say softly, "I understand. Maybe it's for the best you do go because you're the only person I can think of right now. Maybe it's because I'm lonely, frightened and vulnerable but you're the only friend I've got to turn to. Gloria has been amazing, but she doesn't offer me the same support that you do. I'm not being fair on you by keep on asking you to come. Maybe it's for the best that you walk away now, for both our sakes."

He nods and yet stands rooted to the spot. Our eyes connect and I can't look away. He shuffles a little closer and I meet him halfway. He reaches out and I take his hand as he pulls me close and whispers, "I can't walk away, Sarah. I can't let you go."

I look into those kind eyes and feel my heart flutter. I imagine those lips on mine chasing the shadows away and making things better. I crave him like oxygen because he is the only constant in my life. Maybe it's because he's the only person showing me any kindness and I've confused that with something else – a stronger, deeper, connection, that shows my mind's more a mess than I thought it was.

So, I pull back and say sadly, "You should go."

He says nothing and I feel the cold air from outside hit me as the door closes behind him. For a brief moment, I wonder what would have happened if I asked him to stay. Would an already complicated situation be made even more so if I had given in to the impulse to kiss him? What was I thinking? I'm not interested in starting something before this hell I'm in is concluded. Would I really have just gone against every rational thought in my head for one snatched kiss from a kind stranger?

I'm more confused than ever now and pray that sleep comes quickly tonight because I'm not sure how much longer I can cope with this.

Chapter Eighteen

A real man loves his wife, and places his family as the most important thing in life. Nothing has brought me more peace and content in life than simply being a good husband and father. Frank Abagnale

I'm not alone for long.

It must only be around twenty minutes later that I hear a loud knock on the door. I feel nervous as I head across the hall to answer it. Only Gloria and Tony visit, unless you count the unwelcome one from Sylvia. I hope that it's Gloria because I could use someone to talk to after the day I've had already.

However, it's none of the above because standing there, looking slightly agitated, is Mason. I make to slam the door shut, half expecting Sylvia to be behind him but he puts his foot in the way and says desperately, "Please, hear me out, Sarah."

My heart starts racing as I listen to every reason why I should refuse but something about the look in his eyes makes me stop. I recognise that look. I see it in the mirror every day. Mason is struggling and if anyone knows what that's like, it's me.

Against my better judgement, I let him in. He follows me into the kitchen and I say in a dull voice. "I expect you've come to attack me the same as Sylvia. Well, let me save you the job because I don't know where Richard is and I'm not responsible for what happened."

"I know."

I look up in surprise and see the conflict raging through his eyes as he stares at me with a hard expression.

I whisper, "What do you mean… you know?"

He shakes his head and sits down wearily in the same chair that Richard always sat. It shocks me a little to see an older version of my husband sitting where he usually sits, although Mason looks to be a man in torment.

He sighs heavily. "I haven't come here to argue, Sarah. I'm not here to blame you for anything. If anyone knows what my son is capable of, it's me."

I say almost fearfully, "Why are you here then?"

He looks at me with a pitying look and says dully, "Because I believe you."

Those words are unexpected and have more of an effect than any spoken in the last week or so. He believes me. They mean so much coming from a man who should hate me.

He carries on. "We both know that Richard has problems. I recognised the signs from an early age but Sylvia thought he could do no wrong. He was always cruel and unforgiving and having Sylvia as a mother only encouraged him to think he was right. I should have stopped what I saw happening before my own eyes but I was too weak to step in. You see, Sarah, I have also lived my life under the shadow of a formidable partner. Sylvia is the same. She likes to control and does so in a way that strips you of your humanity. I could see the same thing happening to you and I was too weak to step in. Now this is the result and we are going through hell. You see, Richard is our only son and all we have. We need to know what happened and think you can shed light on it. I'm not here to shout or argue or harm you in any way. I'm here for the truth of what happened that night, so we can begin to deal with what that may mean for the future."

I look at him with an overwhelming sadness. Richard is still their son and they must be worried. For all they know, I murdered him and then fled the scene. They must be confused but I know they won't like the answers to their questions.

Sitting opposite him, I say sadly, "You're right. Richard liked to control. He liked obedience and everything was on his terms only. He was a bully and a despicable human being and I was planning on leaving him. You see, I made that decision many years ago but never had the strength to see it through. That night of the accident something snapped inside me and I told him I wanted a divorce."

Mason looks at me and says sadly, "That must have taken a great deal of courage."

I nod. "It was a courage that had deserted me years ago but chose that moment to revisit. I found an inner strength and blurted it out. However, as expected, Richard wasn't having it. He punched me so hard my head hit the window. You see, Mason,

Richard was the one driving, and he caused the accident. When the dust settled, he told me I would pay and fled the scene. He left me to take the blame because I told him I was leaving him. What man does that? A weak, despicable, bully who likes to control everything in his life. Well, that was something he couldn't control, so he took off. If you want to know where he is, it can't be far because your son is still terrorising me now. He is trying to scare me and send me mad but I'm not going to let him. I'm going to do what I should have done years ago and stand up and be counted. You see, Mason, I've had enough and I don't want to be like you and live my life in the shadow of another. He can try but he won't succeed because I have made the decision to be free of him. Whatever happens to me, I will always be free – of him. I may go to prison and I may find things hard but that's the easy part because staying would have been the harshest prison and I owe it to myself to break free."

Mason stands and to my surprise holds out his hand. "I'm sorry, Sarah. I blame myself for not speaking out years ago and sitting back and watching something spiral out of control that I could have prevented. You're not to blame for what happened – I can see that; however, we still need to know where our son is. Sylvia is out of her mind with worry which only spells trouble for me. So, I'm begging you, please tell us any little piece of information that will help us find our son. We need closure on this, for all our sakes."

Turning towards the window, I look outside and see life going on as normal. I see the usual comings and goings of a community wrapped up in their lives without an obvious care in the world. Behind those curtains, a different life may be played out but nobody knows what.

I shake my head and say sadly, "I wish I could help you. Trust me, if I knew where Richard was, I'd be a happier woman. I am locked in a prison awaiting my fate with no control over it. I can assure you that Richard is out there somewhere – watching and waiting. I'm sure that when whatever he's planning pans out you'll have your son back because of that I'm certain. Richard hasn't finished with me yet and I'm resigned to that."

I turn to look at him and say with feeling. "Don't accept your own situation though. You have wasted far too many years already. Find your inner strength and get help for a problem that will never go away. You owe it to yourself to never settle for anything less than you deserve."

Mason stands and says in a low voice. "It's too late for me. You see, this is something you or I come to think of it, will never understand. I love Sylvia. I always have done and even though she treats me this way, I will never leave her, because, without her, I may as well be dead. Maybe you will never understand it, I'm not sure I do but I would rather this life than a life on my own. I admire you, Sarah but I wouldn't want to be in your shoes."

His words shock me and he grins ruefully. "Anyway, I said what I came here to say. Please call me as soon as you hear anything because like I said, we are out of our minds with worry for our son. There is one thing I want to say before I go."

I look at him questioningly and he smiles weakly, "Take care of yourself because I'm not so sure you will be as strong as you think you are. Think about it. In the eyes of the law, you have killed someone, if not two people. You are about to exchange one prison for another and both are unforgiving. If it turns out you did murder our son, there will be no end to your suffering because we will make it our life's work to punish you for what you've done. If it turns out you were right all along, it will probably only be because they find your body because if I know my son and if he is out there, you are about to experience hell on earth and nobody can save you from what he has planned."

He doesn't wait for my reaction and I get no chance to answer him because Mason is gone before I pick my jaw up from the floor. As knockout punches go, that was a good one.

Shaking, I race to the door and bolt the door as tightly as possible. I lean back against it and feel my legs shake with fear and my heart beat out of control. He's right. I'm waiting here for the inevitable and there is no way out. Richard is out there biding his time and I am making it easy for him.

Chapter Nineteen

A real friend is one who walks in when the rest of the world walks out. Walter Winchell

The next few days are uneventful. Nobody calls and the walls are closing in on me. There is no word from Tony which doesn't surprise me. I could tell he wouldn't be back. There was something about the look in his eyes that told me he was walking away. I call my solicitor but she doesn't return my calls. Even Gloria doesn't stop by and I think I'm going out of my mind with boredom and worry.

Then, one morning, I decide to do something different. It's a beautiful day outside and there is a lot of activity in Richmond Avenue. I see James washing his car and various neighbours out tending their gardens. Children are cycling past on their bikes and their happy laughter makes me smile. Life goes on and so should mine. I need to start living again and so, I grab my gardening trug and head outside to join them.

As I take a deep breath, I feel the fresh air fill my lungs and my heart settles. Why didn't I do this weeks ago? I may be waiting for something out of my control but I am allowed outside. I should be making the most of my freedom while I have it and look around me with a little trepidation.

I kneel down to the side of the flower bed and start pulling out the weeds. The birds circle overhead looking for food and the sound of a lawnmower buzzes nearby. Looking up, I see James polishing his car and as he looks in my direction. I raise my hand and wave. He turns away.

I feel a little foolish. Maybe he didn't see me. Carrying on I see Jenny walking along Richmond Avenue towards Alice's house. She looks up and I smile and wave. She, however, looks down and turns away.

A cold feeling creeps over me. What's going on?

Standing up, I move to the edge of my drive and watch Sally and Crispin get into their car. I call out, "Hey, Sally."

The car door slams and the engine starts, cutting any conversation stone dead.

I make to move towards the reversing car and then it happens. I see her. Ellie Matthews, standing across the road behind the reversing car. I watch with horror as she waves and smiles at me. I cry out as the car gains speed and she shakes her head and smiles once more as the car hits. I watch in horror as she flies forward into the road and lies in a heap on the ground.

It all seems so real and yet they drive off and the body disappears. I know it's my mind playing tricks on me but it all seems so real. I pinch myself literally to check I'm not dreaming but nothing changes. Sinking to my knees, I start to cry. This is too much; I'm slowly going mad. What's happening to me?

As I sob on the path outside my house, life in Richmond Avenue goes on. Cars pass me and children play. Sounds of nature mix with those of man and nobody pays me any attention. I am invisible and no longer part of this community. I may as well be dead because this is no life to live.

Then I hear steps running towards me and a gentle hand on my shoulder. "Hey, Sarah. It's ok, I'm here. Let's get you inside."

Looking up, I see Gloria's anxious eyes staring down at me and I smile at her gratefully and say in a whisper, "I think I'm going mad, Gloria."

She shakes her head. "No, you're not, honey. You're the sane one in all of this. Let's get you inside and you can tell me all about it."

She helps me back inside number 15 and I'm grateful when the door closes and peace is restored.

Gloria makes me a cup of tea and says kindly, "Listen, Sarah. There's something you should know."

She smiles sadly. "The people around here are conflicted. Word is, you killed Richard, and it's all they can talk about. Obviously, I believe you and have told them as much but they aren't convinced. The police have taken statements from everyone and you know what they're like, so wrapped up in their own lives they don't want to get involved in another's problems."

I say shakily, "So, they think I'm a murderer."

She nods sadly. "I'm sorry but you know what they're like. They stay away because they don't want to be dragged into all this. I've tried to reason with them but nobody will budge. Until this is resolved, you don't exist. To them anyway. I'm sure you're not surprised, really. I mean, I'd be surprised if they did stand by you to be honest. It's human nature, after all. Friends on the surface but when the chips are down, they stay well away. Too wrapped up in their own lives to give a thought to anyone else. Word is, you're heading to prison, and that scares the hell out of them."

I feel the tears pricking my eyes and say shakily, "They think I murdered Richard?"

She nods and I put my face in my hands and sob loudly. It's too much. Nobody believes me, not even who I once classed as friends.

Gloria places her hand on my back and rubs gently. "There, there, they'll soon learn it was all a misunderstanding. I'm sure when the trial begins the evidence will prove your innocence."

I look at her in anguish. "Are you sure about that, Gloria? I mean, from what I can see, the evidence is pointing to my guilt, not the other way around."

She looks at me sympathetically and I can see it in her eyes. She doesn't believe me. Gloria is the best friend I have ever had and even she doesn't believe me. She strokes my hair as a mother would comfort a child and says warmly, "Listen, I don't have long but when I saw you, I had to come. I'll be back later and take you out somewhere. Maybe to the supermarket. You must be running low by now and I'm sure the odd supplies I keep bringing you aren't your usual choice. Why don't you take a bath, wash your hair, anything to make yourself feel better and hang tight for me? I think you've been holed up in this place long enough, don't you? I mean, it's enough to send anyone crazy."

I nod miserably as she moves towards the back door. "Give me a couple of hours, honey, that's all it will take."

As she heads outside, I think about what she said. Would I think the same way as my neighbours if it was one of them? Probably and that tells me what a shallow world we live in. Richmond Avenue is a great place to live all the time you don't step outside the parallel lines of normality. Mess with those lines at your peril because they will ultimately trip you up in the end.

Sighing, I head off to do as Gloria suggested. Maybe I should take some time to wallow in my own self-pity and make myself feel as normal as I can because I am looking forward to getting out of this place. Gloria has just thrown me a lifeline. A change of scene and non-judgemental people who won't know who I am. Maybe for a couple of hours at least, I can be normal again.

Chapter Twenty

We're born alone, we live alone, we die alone.
Only through our love and friendship can we create
the illusion for the moment that we're not alone.
Orson Welles

Two hours later and there is no sign of Gloria. I've been ready and waiting for close on half an hour but there's no sign of her. I see her coffee coloured car parked in her driveway so she must be home. Gloria isn't the sort to walk anywhere and I've never seen her out for a run.

An hour later and there's still no sign. I feel a little exasperated because I've been pinning so much hope on this brief shopping trip. Just the promise of a fresh scene and an activity as mundane as grocery shopping is starting to mean the world to me and I'm impatient to go. Maybe I should just drive myself. I mean, I'm surprised I never thought of it before. However, the thought of sitting behind a steering wheel again fills me with dread. My car is long gone. It was never returned after the accident and I'm happy about that. I never want to see it again because it killed someone I held dear. The one woman who had everything and because of my own stupidity was left with nothing.

I could take Richard's car but the thought of sitting where he once sat also fills me with dread.

Just touching the wheel is enough to give me a panic attack and being in a closed space of his is too much to bear. It's difficult enough being faced with his clothes hanging in the wardrobe every day. I half expect to see him getting ready as I choose my outfit. Just the sight of his perfectly tailored suits and pristine shirts hanging in order of colour makes me feel dizzy. The smell of his aftershave lingers in the dressing room and his polished leather shoes mock me from their positions on the shelves.

Richard is everywhere I look and yet somehow, I have accepted this part of him. Inanimate objects that tell me he lived here once. Reminding me of the monster within who made me live in fear. I need those reminders to keep me strong to deal with the present because if I allow it, I will fold under this huge pressure. I can feel it. I am living on a fine line between madness and the future. Which way I fall will be the decider, so I need to remain focused and sharp.

Feeling a little stronger, I decide to head next door and see if Gloria's home. I should have done this days ago.

It feels strange venturing outside the perimeter of the house for the first time. It feels wrong and as if I'm doing something I shouldn't. I see nobody as I make the short journey, yet feel as if I'm being watched from behind the twitching curtains.

Feeling my bravery fast deserting me, I try to tell myself I'm doing something I have always done and not to be afraid. I *need* to be strong and I *can* be strong. After all, it's just a brief visit next door.

Reaching the front door, I take a deep breath and ring the doorbell. Somewhere inside I hear voices but no footsteps heading my way. I press the bell again and wait nervously. Once again, five minutes pass and nobody comes.

Feeling irritated I head around the back. There must be someone in. I can hear them.

Reaching the back door, I place my hand on the handle and test it. It turns freely and the door inches open a little more. I call out loudly, "Gloria, it's Sarah, are you in here?"

I hear the voices coming from the room at the front of the house and follow the sound. It feels wrong, like an intruder with no right to be here.

As I reach the room, I see the television playing out noisily and realise the voices I heard came from that. There is nobody here and then I see a familiar image flash on the screen. I recognise the place and my heart stops. Gander Green lane.

I stare at the screen as the reporter's voice tells me everything I need to hear.

Earlier today, Police were called when a dog walker found a man's body in the woods behind Gander Green lane. Early indications are that it's the missing solicitor Richard Standon. Viewers may remember the fatal accident here less than two weeks ago where a local resident, Ellie Matthews, was knocked down and killed by the car driven by Sarah Standon, Richard Standon's wife.

With me is Detective Inspector Jones of the Metropolitan police who is in charge of this case. "What can you tell the viewers of this reported find?"

I watch in disbelief as officer Jones looks into the camera with an extremely grave expression.

"I can confirm that earlier today, a man's body was found in the woods behind us. Forensics' are currently attending the scene and we are trying to identify him. The body looks to be of a similar age and build to the missing solicitor Richard Standon and we are carrying out tests to clarify that."

I step back in shock. Richard? It can't be... can it?

The screen flicks back to the studio and the story changes and I try to think clearly. Could it be Richard? What if he crawled away injured from the scene and died in those woods? But that wouldn't explain the things that have been happening and the phone call – surely.

As I step outside the room, I hear a sound coming from upstairs. I'm not sure why but I move silently towards the stairs. With one hand on the bannisters, I start to move up them slowly and carefully. I should call out, I should walk away, anything but creep around where I don't belong. However, something is compelling me to discover what it is. The voices get louder with each step I take. I hear a woman's moans and my heart rate increases. Gloria.

I hear banging which reminds me of the headboard as Richard thrust inside me angrily, brutally, like a feral beast. The moans turn to groans and I stop. This is wrong. It must be Gloria with her fitness trainer. It's probably why she had to get back. Even I know nothing gets in the way of her workout with him.

The trouble is, my mind is telling me to walk away but I can't. I know it's wrong but I need to know. As I inch towards the landing, I hear her cry out which brings me to my senses. I need to leave.

I turn away and run silently, stealthily, back the way I came. My heart hammers as I flee the scene with all the images swirling around my mind from what I've learned inside this house.

Without another thought, I head towards the back door. Then I see it and it stops me in my tracks.

Hanging on the back of the wooden chair at the table is a familiar sight. One I would know from any other because of the stitching inside the neck. The custom silk lining that brands it as his. Richard's jacket. Not the tracksuit of a personal trainer. Not Edward's usual pilot's uniform. Richard's tailored jacket that costs more than our monthly mortgage payment, hanging on the back of Gloria's chair while she entertains him upstairs.

I feel sick and my head spins as I charge outside. Taking a deep breath, I flee the scene and don't stop running until I'm safely inside the house. Bolting the door, I race to the hallway and grab the phone before racing to the window overlooking Gloria's house. Shakily, I dial Tony's number and wait for him to answer, all the time watching for Richard to leave the house next door.

The phone switches to voicemail and I say breathlessly, "Please, Tony, it's Sarah Standon. Please, can you come? I think Richard's next door."

I hang up and then try again. Still, no answer and so I try again. I keep on trying with one eye on the street outside. He's in there. I know he is.

In frustration, I turn my attention to the local police station and call the number instead. A voice says sternly, "Hayes-Standing police station. How may I help you?"

I say breathlessly, "Please can someone come. I'm Sarah Standon at number 15 Richmond Avenue. My husband, Richard is missing and they think it's his body on Gander Green lane. I think he's in the house next door, number 14 Richmond Avenue."

There's a brief silence, and the operator says firmly, "The officers are on their way. Please, can you confirm your identity?"

I whisper, "Sarah Standon. His wife. Please hurry, I know it's him."

She reassures me, "The officers are on their way and I will notify the officer in charge of the case."

With shaking hands, I replace the phone and stare at the house next door. Gloria and Richard. Of course. Why am I so blind? The screams start in my

mind as the memory I have tried so hard to erase
revisits me.

Chapter Twenty-One

Nearly all men can stand adversity, but if you want to test a man's character, give him power.
Abraham Lincoln

Four years earlier.

Richard wants something. I can tell by the way he is looking at me. He smiles sexily as he dresses in his black jeans that hug his body and make my mouth water. He pulls a tight-fitting top over his broad, muscular body and my breath hitches. His eyes flash as he stares at me with the look that always brings me to my knees. Pure, sexual desire. His eyes have a spark to them tonight. He is excited I can tell and I smile. "You look happy, darling."

He nods and walks towards me and I feel my heart race. He runs his hand around my waist and pulls me close and whispers, "I'm looking forward to tonight, baby."

I laugh softly. "What, dinner with the neighbours?"

He smiles. "Among other things."

Shaking my head, I feel the desire inside as he lowers his mouth to my neck. A gentle nip and then a suck and I'm putty in his hands. He groans, "You look good enough to eat my darling. I am going to enjoy showing you something different tonight."

I'm almost tempted to ditch our plans this evening and tell him to make our excuses but it's Gloria's birthday. We've been invited to share the occasion and to my knowledge are the only ones so it would be rude to let her down. Richard laughs softly. "You know how happy you make me, baby."

I nod, feeling the delicious thrill flood through me that marriage to this man always brings. "Same for me, darling. You have made me the happiest woman on earth."

His lips find mine and I kiss my husband as if I can't get enough and I can't. I can never get enough of Richard. I still pinch myself that I'm married to such a wonderful man. A man that makes my pulse race and my heart sing. A man that fulfils me in every way and I can't live without. I am the luckiest woman in the world.

He pulls back and winks and grabs hold of my hand.

"We had better go now before this goes the way it always does. Save this moment, baby because it promises great rewards later."

Shivering in anticipation, I follow him from the dressing room. A woman in love and blind to any flaws that may reveal themselves. Richard can do no wrong in my eyes, he never could.

Edward answers the door and smiles his welcome. "Good to see you, come in. The birthday girl is knocking back the champagne already."

Richard slaps him on the back and says loudly, "Good to see you, Ed. This promises to be a night to remember."

I'm not sure why but his words surprise me. I wonder what they have up their sleeve because they share a look that confuses me. They have a secret and by the look in their eyes, it's one they can't wait to get out in the open.

As we follow Edward, I whisper, "What's going on, have you got a surprise for Gloria?"

Richard winks. "All in good time."

Shaking my head, I follow them into the kitchen where Gloria is setting out plates of food on the table. "Hey, guys, good to see you."

She smiles excitedly and moves across to kiss us on the cheeks. I say warmly, "Happy birthday, Gloria, you're looking lovely tonight."

She laughs self-consciously. "Not bad for someone turning thirty."

Edward slips his arm around her shoulders and pulls her close, dropping a light kiss on the top of her head.

"She's still my sexy 21-year-old."

Gloria giggles and I watch slightly embarrassed as he kisses her deeply, a long, lingering, kiss that appears to go on forever. Sneaking a look at Richard, I see him watching them with a strange look in his eyes. For the first time in their company, I feel uncomfortable.

After what seems like ages, they pull back and Gloria rolls her eyes. "Sorry guys. What can I say, I married a beast?"

I laugh nervously and Edward looks at me and smirks and something about the look in his eyes sets me on edge. Trying to shake a bad feeling, I say brightly, "Let me help you, Gloria. You shouldn't be working on your birthday."

She smiles, and we set about laying out the food. It all looks delicious and they have obviously gone to a great deal of trouble. Richard and Edward drift off with beers in hand and occasionally I hear loud laughter coming from their direction.

Gloria shakes her head. "Look at them. A couple of grown-up kids if ever I saw them."

Laughing, I have to agree. There is a lightness of spirit to them tonight. They are carefree and excitable and I'm happy to see it. I smile. "Yes, it's good to see Richard having fun. He works so hard and doesn't get much time to relax and chill. It's good to see."

Gloria smiles. "You're so lucky, Sarah. You have it all. Beautiful home, good looks and fantastic clothes. And as for that husband of yours, he's something else entirely. He could be a movie star or something, he has that look about him."

I nod, feeling a little smug as I see the jealousy in her eyes. Yes, Richard is a catch, I've always known that. I see the envy in the other women's eyes as they follow him around the room. I see the covetous looks and feel my heart fill to bursting.

He's mine, all mine and I'm the luckiest girl on the planet.

We sit down to eat and talk about the usual things. Neighbours, work, holidays. The usual conversation that neighbours share and all the time the alcohol flows freely. I relax in the company of good people, good food and good wine and feel a warm glow of contentment as I thoroughly enjoy my evening.

At first, I don't notice anything strange. A lingering glance from Edward that lasts a fraction of a second longer than it should. A brief touch from Gloria as she brushes imaginary food from my lips with her thumb. The pressure of Richard's leg against mine, causing the desire to increase as I feel his hard body against me. The brush of a foot against my ankle and the seductive music causing a change in the atmosphere. The temperature increases in the room and Edward says lightly, "Shall we take our drinks into the other room?"

I should have taken more notice of the looks they all shared. I certainly noticed them but pushed them away as nothing. I grab hold of my glass and follow them to the hallway and then look with surprise as they head for the stairs. Looking at Richard in confusion, I can see a change in him immediately. As Gloria and Edward made to walk up the stairs, Richard grabs my hand and whispers, "Trust me, Sarah."

I say in confusion. "What do you mean?"

He says in a low voice. "Follow my lead and you will have the night of your life."

I think the realisation hits me hard because I stumble back and say in a low voice, "No."

His expression changes immediately and he grabs my wrist and growls, "You will do as I say or suffer the consequences. Trust me, Sarah. I won't let any harm come to you."

He pushes me towards the stairs and I stumble.

I hold on to the bannisters and say fearfully, "I can't do this - I won't do this."

Richard snarls, "Don't make me angry. You won't like what that means."

Gloria stands at the top of the stairs and looks worried. "Is everything ok?"

Edward looks at Richard and says, "I thought you said she'd agree."

I shout, "No, I don't want to. I'm going home."

Turning away, I make towards the door and the silence follows me out. I walk home alone. I let myself inside and run sobbing upstairs. I can't believe what just happened. What they wanted me to do. I'm not a fool, I saw where this evening was ending up. I can't believe Richard wanted me to be part of whatever they had planned.

I sit sobbing on the bathroom floor, alone, confused and slightly afraid. Richard doesn't come back for several hours and it must be early morning before I fall into a fitful sleep.

When I wake, it's with Richard sitting beside me looking so angry it takes my breath away.

"You selfish bitch."

I make to sit up but he pushes me down forcibly and holds my wrists in his hands and I feel the burn. He snarls, "How could you show me up like that in public? You ruined everything, Sarah, and you only have yourself to blame."

I say fearfully, "What do you mean, I can't believe you wanted me to do… that?"

"What Sarah? Do what? Drag your mind from the gutter and just think for a moment. What did you think was going to happen last night?"

I look at him in confusion. "But I thought…"

He laughs darkly, "Oh I know what you thought and it just shows you what a sick, twisted, mind, you've got. It was embarrassing. Seeing my wife running from the room like a frightened rabbit. Trying to explain why my own damn wife was afraid of her own shadow. Trying to rescue something from the mess you caused when you left the party. Well, it showed me just what a weak minded individual I married. Do you have anything to say to me, Sarah?"

I stare at him in shock and confusion. "But… I thought."

He laughs darkly. "I know what you thought. You thought I wanted to share you. You're sick, Sarah. You know that, don't you?"

I feel the shame wash over me as I realise what an assumption I made. I say shakily, "I'm so sorry Richard."

He releases me as if the very touch of me disgusts him. "You'll have to do a lot more than that to make it up to me. You will have to beg for my forgiveness because I am so disappointed in the woman I married; I'm fast considering my options."

I feel the tears running like rivers down my face as I plead, "I'm so sorry, darling. I didn't mean to run out on you, I just thought."

He turns away in disgust. "I know what you thought. I'm going to the office and you can think about dragging your mind out of the gutter and turn your attention to how you will make it up to me."

I watch helplessly as he storms out and in a matter of seconds, I hear the angry roar of his car engine as he leaves for the day.

For the rest of the day, I'm in shock. How did I get things so badly wrong? He's right. I embarrassed him in front of our friends and god only knows what they must think.

Feeling utterly bereft, I make up a posy of flowers from the garden and take them next door.

Gloria opens the door and looks at me with a sad expression and I say nervously, "I'm sorry about last night, Gloria. I don't know what came over me. Maybe it was the alcohol or lack of sleep but I should never have run out."

She smiles thinly and nods. "It's ok, Sarah. Richard told us you were feeling stressed. Do you want to talk about it?"

She stands aside and nods for me to follow and I head inside meekly. As she puts the kettle on, she says softly, "You know, there was nothing sinister in what happened last night. Edward had surprised me by turning the spare room into a home cinema. We spent the rest of the evening curled up in there watching movies. You missed a great night."

Her words make me more ashamed than ever and I say apologetically, "I'm so sorry, Gloria. I made an assumption that was out of order. I'm sorry to ruin your birthday."

She looks at me a little strangely and says softly, "Trust me, honey. I had the night of my life."

As she turns away, I brush away her words along with the memory of the night before.

However, my life was never the same from that day onwards. Richard changed overnight, and I spent the rest of our married life walking on eggshells and trying to regain what we once had. It began.

Chapter Twenty-Two

Growth is painful. Change is painful. But, nothing is as painful as staying stuck where you do not belong. N. R. Narayana Murthy

Now I sit waiting for the police to revisit the house where it all started. They don't take long. I see the police car stop outside number 14 and two officers get out. One walks to the front door and one to the rear and my heart settles – a little.

I think I hold my breath as the door opens and I see the officer say something. I can't hear a thing as the officer heads inside and I feel my heart thumping as I wait. I think he must be inside for ten minutes before the two officers leave – empty-handed.

I shake my head. Surely, they searched the place. Somebody was in there – I heard it with my own ears and I definitely saw Richard's jacket on the chair. I'm positive I did.

I watch the officers make their way to my door and my heart starts beating furiously as they ring the doorbell.

The look in their eyes tells me what I already know. They found nothing. One of the officers clears his throat and says awkwardly, "Sarah Standon?"

I nod and he carries on.

"We understand you believe your husband is next door."

I nod and say with a whisper, "Yes."

They share a look and one of them says kindly, "We have searched the premises and found only the owners, Gloria and Edward Sullivan."

I stare at them in surprise. "But it can't be Edward. His car isn't there, and I saw my husband's jacket on the chair."

One of them says, "So you were in the house?"

I nod weakly, "Yes."

Once again, they share a look and one of them says kindly, "Maybe you were mistaken. I understand you've been under a considerable amount of strain lately. Your mind can play tricks on you when that happens. I would rest and try to relax if I were you."

There's nothing else to say. They don't believe me and that feeling is hard to accept. I watch as another car arrives and my heart sinks as I see officer Jones heading my way. The two other officers turn and greet him before heading off and he says sharply, "May I come inside, Sarah?"

I nod miserably. "Yes, of course."

Unlike Tony, officer Jones is scary. He never smiles and looks at me as if I'm the last person he wants to be around. He sighs heavily. "We found a man's body in the woods behind Gander Green lane."

I hold my breath as I wait for the news.

He exhales sharply. "We are waiting for them to identify him but we have reason to believe it's your husband. He's the same height, build and age but his face is badly battered and unrecognisable. Before we get the confirmation, is there anything you would like to say? If you withhold anything, it will work against you in the long run. This is your chance to say what happened and set the record straight before we discover it for ourselves."

I sink down onto the settee and put my head in my hands. "Do you think it's him?"

I feel the seat next to me sag as he sits down and says in a strangely gentle voice, "I think it is. I think that you had a fight that night. It happens, it's not unusual. I'm guessing it got out of hand and maybe, just maybe, he was injured by accident. I believe you must have panicked and fled the scene. He was probably still alive and followed you out and you took off in the car. I'm guessing he was also in that car and you struck out again. Eye-witness reports show the car was swaying from side to side, which would explain the fight inside. I'm guessing when you crashed, you were preoccupied with the scene and he crawled away. Maybe he was disorientated and had a wound his body couldn't sustain. Am I right, Sarah? Is that what happened because if it was, you can rest assured you will be dealt with sympathetically? The courts will bear in mind it was an accident but you have to tell us what happened."

I look at him in fear. "But what if it isn't him? What if he's still out there because I know he is?

I'm not sure who that man is you've found because my husband is stalking me now. He called me and is torturing me at night. Strange things have been happening here and it can only be because he's still alive. I know he was next door because I saw his jacket. I know I heard his voice on the phone and I can't explain why everything's been put in my name. Please officer Jones, please believe me when I say Richard isn't dead and he's coming for me."

I stare at him willing him to believe me and he sighs with exasperation. "Very well. If that's how you want to play it, I'll leave you in peace. However, I will return. As soon as the body's identified, I'll be back with a warrant for your arrest. Something happened that night and you know what. Maybe you should search deep within your soul and put your husband's family out of their misery. They are in Hell over this and only you have the answers they need."

He says no more and heads back the way he came leaving me a quivering wreck. I know that body isn't Richard. How can it be?

Gloria doesn't return and I don't blame her. I called the police to her door and she must think I'm mad. I feel on edge and can't sit still. This whole situation is bad and I can see no way out. Nobody believes me and I've alienated the one remaining friend I had. I start to feel angry. This isn't right. I did nothing but put up with years of abuse from a dangerous man. I won't let him win - I can't.

With determination, I head upstairs and start pulling his clothes from the closet. I throw them in a heap on the floor and once I start, I can't stop. One by one, his immaculate suits and shirts are reduced to piles of crushed fabric. I fling his shoes down the stairs and relish the sound of them bouncing off the walls and spilling onto the floor below. Then I take his shampoo and pour it down the plughole, closely followed by his aftershave. I bag up all his personal possessions with no care or regard into rubbish bags.

I am going to extinguish him from my life once and for all until there is nothing left of him. I don't want him in my life anymore; I haven't for some time. Richard needs to die to me because all the time I let him control me with fear he will win. I'm taking it back and it starts right here with all his possessions.

I work through every room in the house. I smash photographs and take great delight in destroying what took years to put together. I laugh like a madwoman as I destroy all evidence of him in my home. Because when all is said and done, it is *my* home. Not his, for whatever reason he made it this way and now I will take advantage of his own stupidity. Systematically, I destroy every trace of my husband and it feels liberating.

Once I reach the office, I upturn drawers and rake through cupboards. His treasured possessions find their way to the trash and I feel my soul cleansing as I work. This is what I should have done in the first place. I need him out of my life once and for all and it starts here.

I work long into the night, removing every last trace of the man I now despise. Once I am sure his worldly possessions are out in the trash, I start to scrub. I work until my fingers ache as I remove every last trace of him from this house. The bedding is washed, and the towels disposed of. I only keep the guest ones because he never touched those. All the time I play the loudest rock music that he hates with a passion. The sounds of Iron Maiden and Nickelback calm my soul as I relish how much he would hate it.

The sun is coming over the horizon when the last trace of him is dealt with. Far from being tired, I am invigorated. A new day in a new life. Whatever happens next, I am free of him forever.

At 6 am on the first day of the rest of my life, I fall into a deep, contented, sleep.

At 6 pm, I wake up in hell.

Chapter Twenty-Three

Expose yourself to your deepest fear; after that, fear has no power, and the fear of freedom shrinks and vanishes. You are free. Jim Morrison

I wake with aching muscles as a result of a solid, deep, sleep. As I stretch out in contentment, I feel a lightness to my spirit that hasn't been present for some time. Sighing, I turn in the bed and stretch my limbs, enjoying the feeling that only a deep sleep gives you. Looking over to the bedside table, I see the digital display of the alarm clock announcing its 6 pm. I have slept for twelve hours. I can't remember the last time I indulged in such luxury and I smile softly to myself as I feel my heart settle.

"Hello, Sarah."

The fear returns with a vengeance and grabs hold of my fragile heart, threatening to shatter it into a million pieces. The voice that speaks leaves me with a cold feeling that wraps me in disbelief. Richard.

I bolt from the bed as if it's on fire and stare in disbelief at the shadowy figure sitting in the chair by the open window. The cool breeze makes the curtains billow as I blink in the hope I'm having a nightmare.

He laughs hollowly and says in a deep voice. "It's time to make you pay for what you did, Sarah."

Nervously, I look to the door, my only exit and watch as he moves to block it. My legs start shaking as I run my tongue around my drying lips and whisper, "How did you get in?"

He laughs bitterly. "Is that all you've got to say? How did I get in? I thought you may have a smarter question than that. Mind you, you've always been as dumb as shit. Maybe that's why you lasted as long as you did."

Swallowing hard, I try to think of a way to keep him talking until I can work out a plan of escape. I shiver as the cool breeze hits my skin and say, "Where have you been?"

He smiles, but it has no warmth. "I've been watching you, Sarah. I've been waiting for my plan to pan out and now it's time to end this charade."

I say louder. "You never answered my question. Where have you been?"

His eyes flash and his voice cuts across the room like a knife. "I have never left, you stupid bitch. You thought you were so clever getting your policeman friend to search this house. You thought you were safe in the home I provided for us both and you thought I was otherwise occupied next door. How I laughed at your confusion. How I enjoyed watching you turn slightly mad as I pulled your strings. Because that's what you are and always have been to me – a puppet."

He starts to advance, slowly, carefully and with promise and I swallow hard. Edging back towards the wall, I say weakly, "Don't do this. This must end. *We* must end. We killed a woman and if anything, make that your revenge. I will tell them I was driving if you leave - now."

His laugh is cruel, much like the man himself, as he growls, "I haven't finished with you yet. We have a lot to talk about you and I. Tonight is our chance to get it all out in the open. Put our marriage to bed as they say and move on with our lives."

I feel my heart beating frantically as he steps before me and reaches out, grabbing my wrist hard and pulling me close. He sneers, "You were always weak. It was easy for me to wear you down and make you do everything I wanted. You were so desperate to hang onto me. I knew you couldn't believe your luck when I chose you. I saw the envious looks of your so-called friends who would betray you in an instant for one night in my bed. They were never your friends because it was always *me*. Always me they wanted, craved in fact and you were just the means to get my attention."

He pulls me closer and I smell the familiar scent of toothpaste on his breath. His lips crash onto mine and his tongue plunders my mouth. Biting, searching, punishing, his kiss is as brutal as the man himself. Pulling back, he grips my hair in his fist and says darkly, "You need to think about what you've done, Sarah."

I start to cry as the full horror of my situation reveals itself. I start to shake. "No, please Richard. I promise you I'll never tell, just please leave me alone."

His laughter banishes any hope I have left as he pulls me from the room. I stumble as he marches along the hall with one destination in mind. The punishment room.

Kicking out, I catch him briefly off guard and as his grip loosens, I make a run for it. I feel my heart beating as I take the stairs three at a time and feel him gaining on me as I head for the panic button. I never make it. He grabs my hair and pulls me back causing the tears to fall from my eyes as he hisses, "Naughty, naughty, you have earned a harsher punishment."

He drags me by my hair into the large living space and slams my head against the wall. I swear I see stars as I fall to the ground and he steps back. "Is this what you want, to fight? Because if it is, I am only too willing."

Shaking my head, I look up and then around me in disbelief. Everything I cleared away has been returned. It looks as if we've been burgled as I see the broken frames amid upturned plants. Tables on their side and broken lamps. The room is exactly as I saw it the first time I returned with the officers after the accident and I start shaking uncontrollably.

Richard looks around and laughs. "Does this look familiar, darling. I must say standards have slipped since I let you out on your own. Maybe you should start by cleaning this mess up and restoring my house to what I expect."

With purpose, he reaches down and grabs me by the hair again and grinds my face into the dirt on the floor. A broken piece of glass from the frame pierces my skin and I cry out in agony. "No."

He laughs again and kicks me hard in the ribs. As I gasp for breath, he sneers, "Not much of a fighter, are you? I always knew you were weak and you have just proved that."

He pulls me up and pushes me against an upturned table. The elevated wooden leg catches me in the side and I cry out in pain. I feel him reach for my arm and pull it behind my back and it feels as if it's about to snap as he snarls, "I am going to enjoy punishing you all night long, Sarah."

Blindly, I try to wriggle free which only excites him more. He kicks my legs apart and I crash to the floor again. As my head spins, I know he intends to kill me tonight. There will be no escaping him this time. His eyes hold murderous intent and I must fight for my life if I'm to survive. If I can just raise the alarm, I will be saved.

In a rasping voice, I say, "You win Richard, I'm sorry. Do whatever you want because I don't have any strength left to fight."

His laughter tells me he's won. He is too strong for me and it's only as he turns to grab my leg and pull me across the floor towards the stairs that I see my chance. My breasts graze against the carpet as he drags me across the broken glass and debris littering the floor. As I pass the upturned table in the hallway, I grab hold of the paperweight that has fallen nearby. He doesn't see it as he strides to the stairs intent on pulling me up them. I have no dignity left. Naked and bleeding and bruised so much it hurts. He pulls me like a rag doll across the once pristine home and it's only when he pulls me up to push me forward, I seize my chance. Putting the full force of any power I have left behind it; I swing the paperweight and bring it down hard on the back of his head and hear the crunch of bone as he howls in agony. Stumbling back, he falls against the wall and I reach blindly for the panic alarm.

As I launch myself onto it, I feel a sharp pain travel through me like an electric shock and I must pass out because the next thing I know, I'm in the punishment room.

Chapter Twenty-Four

Positivity, confidence, and persistence are key in life, so never give up on yourself. Khalid

My hands and legs are tied to each corner of the bed but this time, I'm on my back. I can see everything and my heart freezes as I see Richard staring at me from the corner of the room. Blood is still dripping from his head where I hit him and he has the look of a man possessed. He laughs darkly as he sees I'm awake.

"Nice of you to join me, Sarah. Now the fun can really begin."

My lips are parched and I taste the metallic taste of my own blood as I say pleadingly, "Please Richard. Give this up. The alarm's been raised and the police will be here any second. If anything, run while you still can."

He looks amused which confuses me.

"You think your boyfriend is going to ride in and rescue you? Don't make me laugh. That panic alarm is as useless as you are. Don't think I haven't thought of everything because you know me better than that. Maybe you felt a little pain when you pressed it my darling. That was just a little, shall we say, shock, to remind you who controls who around here. You see, baby, it was always about control."

He crosses the room and I feel the bed sag under his weight as he sits astride me, and the look in his eyes tell me he has now gone completely mad. He starts to stroke my hair and whispers, "I wanted you my darling because you were perfect for me in every way. Good, kind and pliable. Somebody not too confident who would challenge me. Somebody who was a little insecure and needed me to make them complete. A woman I could mould into my perfect image of one and show my mother I was better than her."

His face contorts in a twisted rage as he spits her name like venom on his tongue. I say gently, "Is this why you did this... to prove something to your mother?"

He shakes his head. "All my life that woman controlled me. I can't remember a time she didn't. Both my father and I existed for her own pleasure. But we were never good enough. There was nothing either of us could ever do that gained her approval. You see, that woman had standards so high nobody could ever reach them. If she was displeased, you soon knew about it and this punishment room was a five-star hotel to what she provided."

He breaks off and I think I hold my breath as I see the pain in his eyes. His breathing comes hard and fast as he is transported back to a childhood he never really escaped from.

He looks at me and I see the fear in his eyes as he says roughly. "I tried so hard but I was never good enough. I studied and reached the top of my class. I never fought with the other boys and did my homework on time. I never answered back and kept my room tidy but she was never happy. Even if I ate in the wrong way, she would punish me. She would grind my face into the plate and then leave me to clear it away. If I even spoke in a way she didn't like, she would whip my ass until I couldn't sit down."

I catch my breath and say softly, "I'm so sorry. No child should live like that."

He looks at me in confusion. "What do you mean, *every* child should live like that? She taught me to be strong, Sarah. She showed me that weakness is punished and strength rewarded. She showed me how a mother's love is hard for a reason because she loved me. She told me every day even when she punished me because that was how amazing she was. She had so much love in her heart it pained her to punish me. She loved me so much she made it her life's work to make me into a successful man who could provide a decent home for his family."

I watch as the anger enters his eyes again as he hisses, "I wanted that for us. I wanted to be even half a father as she was a mother. I wanted to shape you into the perfect wife and mother to show her that it mattered. All of it mattered. The endless beatings and emotional torture. The starvation and the mind games counted for something because she was right all along. I had learned the valuable lesson she wanted me to learn and I could finally make her proud."

He starts to shake me as the anger takes hold. "You couldn't be that person, could you? You had to ruin everything by challenging me at every turn. You couldn't even provide me with a family to show her I had succeeded. You were weaker than me and I hate you for it. If you are looking to blame anyone for your situation, my darling, look in the mirror."

He presses down on my heart and I feel the pressure building. The pain is excruciating and I cry out. Releasing me he strides across the room and shouts angrily, "This is all your fault and now you will pay. You are the one who will remember that day forever because you are the one who caused it to happen. We were happy until you decided you wanted more. Like the greedy whore you are, it was never enough. Now everything is ruined because of YOU!"

He grabs a flashlight off the side and directs its beam into my eyes. I blink as the harsh, white, light, hits me and he shouts, "Look at the light, Sarah because you have created a world of darkness. I have lived in this world for so long and wanted us both to find the light together. Well, now is that time because it's time."

I say fearfully, "What do you mean, it's time?"

He sneers. "It's time to end this. Time to move on and we will do it together. Just like we were always meant to. It's always been about us and nobody else. Do you remember that night of Gloria's birthday all those years ago?"

I think I hold my breath as he comes and sits beside me. He reaches out and strokes my body, caressing it like a favourite pet. His breathing intensifies and his eyes darken with desire. "That night I was going to show you the beauty of what my love could do. I was going to introduce to a world where pleasure mingled with pain and made you feel so alive you will crave that feeling forever. Gloria and Edward were going to join us and we were all going to share in the beauty of love. You see, I loved you that much. I was happy to see another man taste you, feel you and enter you and show you how great love could be when it's multiplied. I was willing to share you to give you so much pleasure you would crave it like a drug. You see, that was how generous I was my darling. I only thought of you and your needs. But you had to ruin it by letting the fear dictate your reasoning. You ran away like the frightened little girl you always were, reluctant to expand your mind and see something beautiful."

He starts to laugh like a madman. "Well, you weren't going to spoil my fun. You see, Edward and I had planned it and Gloria got to reap the rewards, while you cowered on the floor in our bedroom in fear. She got to experience the pleasure of love while you just got the pain. You see, Gloria is more of a woman than you'll ever be and she, shall we say, became addicted to what he had to give her.

You may recall her speaking of her personal trainer, well, that was me, Sarah. I was Byron to her, and we spent years indulging in our new favourite hobby. You see, Edward loved her so much he was willing to share; to give her the pleasure she deserved. How does it feel knowing that all the time we met up with our so-called friends, I was more intimate with two of them than my own wife? She owned my heart in a much more meaningful way than you ever could. You see, she trusted us to know what was best for her. She got all the pleasure, all the delights and a life of ecstasy, while you got the pain. How we used to laugh about that."

The tears fall like acid rain down my face as I see the bigger picture. The envious glances and the furtive looks they shared. The pity in her eyes as she almost failed to meet mine and then the shoulder to lean on when it came to it.

I say in a voice that had the emotion stripped from it a long time ago. "Then why was she the only friend I had when I needed it?"

He shrugs. "I don't know, guilt perhaps. Maybe she felt sorry for you like most people did. You see, you were so blind you always thought people envied you. They saw you scurrying after me like a frightened mouse and that envy soon turned to pity. Pity for me, actually. Why would I continue to drag behind me a woman who didn't measure up? A woman who had no backbone of her own and did everything I said. I told them about your mental condition and they pitied me. They felt sorry for the fact I was stuck with a barren wife who was desperate to conceive. A woman who was emotionally dead and yet I stuck by her side. Is it any wonder those women thought I was the perfect catch? This started years ago, Sarah. I have spun such a web you will suffocate in it. Nobody will believe your story because they think you're mad. Sick in the head and they think ultimately you killed your husband."

He presses his fingers down on my throat and I gasp for air. I struggle to breathe as the world turns hazy. His voice floats across the room as the world begins to spin. "Now I cease to exist because of YOU! Richard Standon is no more because I am about to be re-born. You, on the other hand, you will pay the ultimate price because I am sending you straight to Hell."

He releases me and I gasp for oxygen. As I refocus, I see him standing at the foot of the bed, dousing himself with a petrol can. The smell of it makes me gag and the fear slices through my body as I stare into the eyes of a madman. Then I watch in disbelief as he produces a lighter from his pocket. I shout in alarm, "Oh my god, Richard, NO! What are you doing?"

He laughs darkly, "I'm ending this once and for all and you will watch me burn. You will see what you did and lie there thinking about it until the flames claim you to join me in Hell. You see, my darling, I told you I would never let you go. You don't get to be the one to choose and you don't get to leave me. I decide what happens in your life and I choose – death."

I watch helplessly as the spark from the lighter dances in the darkness. The one remaining spark of hope and life in the room and then I watch in disbelief as it ignites the flames. Then I start to scream as Richard's body burns before my very eyes. An all-encompassing flame of destruction as he ends a bitter, twisted, life of pain and anger.

Chapter Twenty-Five

Death is not the greatest loss in life. The greatest loss is what dies inside us while we live - Norman Cousins

My screams turn silent as the smoke invades my body. The rancid smell of burning flesh and the heat of an inferno burns right through me. The bitter smoke replaces oxygen in my lungs and I gasp for breath.

I try so hard to survive a nightmare that threatens to end my life today. The will to live is strong and I give it everything I've got. The dark, dense, choking smoke, obscures my vision and sucks the life from my soul. Then, from somewhere in the distance, I hear *her* voice. The one person who I should never have turned my back on – my mother.

"Don't give up Sarah, please come back to me."

I think time stands still as I try to escape the horror of my situation and focus on the person whose voice is like a light bringing me to shore from a turbulent sea. It's so faint but rings out through the madness as she pleads, "Please darling, don't leave me, I couldn't bear it now that I've found you again."

It almost feels as if she's touching me. A cool hand quenching my searing flesh. A gentle stroke of my hair and the soft touch of a mother who has been lost to me for five long years. Then, I hear another voice, a strong, familiar, voice that brings tears to my eyes. "She moved. Monica, I swear I saw her finger move."

I strain to hear the voice I crave. The one who always made things better and chased the shadows away. My father.

"I saw it, Bill, you're right. Sarah, darling, can you hear us? It's mum and dad, we're here sweetheart, come back to us, open your eyes, you can do this."

My eyelids flicker and I hear another voice say firmly, "Sarah, if you can hear me, please try to nod, a movement, anything."

That voice is also familiar to me, one I never thought I'd hear again – Tony. I'm confused. My parents are here, did Tony fetch them? What about Richard? The fear grips me like a vice and my breathing intensifies. I feel a sudden pain in my arm as Tony says with some urgency, "She's in distress, stand clear."

I don't understand what's happening as something calms me, chasing the shadows away. I hear my mother speak with a tremor in her voice as she pleads, "Fight it, Sarah, fight to live."

I try so hard. Harder than I ever have before to open my eyes but it's as if they have lead weights on them holding them down. My world is dark and full of shadows but I can hear them more clearly now. I feel a touch to my head, a hand stroking my arm. I battle so hard and as one of my eyelids open just a fraction, a sliver of light enters my world. My mother cries, "Bill, doctor, she's coming round, I saw her eyelid flicker."

The voices get louder as they all start talking at once. My head feels so heavy and the pain is like a knife attack. My lips feel dry and I taste an unfamiliar taste in my mouth. Something cool wets my lips and I'm grateful for it. I try again to open my eyes and this time the other one opens allowing a little more light in. It almost blinds me and I start to panic as I fear the flashlight of before. I feel my whole-body trembling as my mother cries out, "Somebody help her, please help my poor baby."

I feel an urgency in the room that wasn't there before. More voices, increasing in volume as my body goes into a spasm. A warm feeling brings life back to my frozen limbs and I *feel* again. The spasm subsides and I feel weak and my limbs ache. My eyes snap open as if in shock and the light blinds me once again. I shake my head and then try again. This time my eyes adjust and a face swirls into view. I feel afraid and whisper silently, "Richard."

"She spoke, did you hear that doctor, she spoke. I heard her."

My mother's voice sounds incredulous, agitated and so emotional, I feel the tears well in my eyes. She's here. She came for me. But how?

It must have been the panic alarm. They saved me.

As I focus, I see her worried face staring at me and I begin to cry like a child. My mum. How I've missed her. Why did I ever let Richard keep me from seeing them? Her tears fall much like mine and she whispers, "I love you, Sarah. Don't worry about a thing darling because you're safe now."

I see my father's anxious face beside her and he says with a catch to his voice. "We're here, baby girl. Nothing can harm you now."

Then I see Tony which confuses me because he is dressed in a doctor's coat. He is looking at me with a kind expression and says, "It's ok, Sarah. You're in the hospital. Do you understand?"

I nod but they are wrong. This was no accident. This was deliberate. Richard tried to kill me and now he is dead.

I try to move but I can't. Am I still tied to that bed, is this all just a dream wishful thinking that I have been saved from the horror? My limbs are like lead weights and Tony says softly, "Don't try to move, one step at a time."

I relax, surely this is happening. I can't be dreaming this, can I?

I take a deep breath and try to speak. My voice comes out weak and soft as I say, "Richard?"

The tears stream from my mother's eyes as she shares a look with my father. She hesitates and then looks at Tony who nods. Taking my hand, she says softly, "He didn't make it, darling. I'm sorry."

I stare at her as if checking her words were real. Can Richard really be dead, or is this some sick twist in his dark plan?

My father says, "I'm sorry darling. Richard never made it but you must fight to come back to us."

So, it's true. He's gone. I'm safe, but how?

For a while, I lie in the hospital bed trying to make sense of what's happening. Gradually things start to come into focus and the life returns to my body. I feel so incredibly weak and ache all over but I'm alive and I'm safe.

Hours pass and my parents sit beside me just talking softly and holding my hands. As they talk, I listen but nothing makes sense, to me anyway.

Tony comes and goes along with my solicitor which is strange because why would she be here dressed as a nurse? The whole situation is so confusing and feels as if I'm in the most ridiculous dream.

Later that evening, I learn the truth.

I am finally allowed to sit up in the hospital bed and have even managed several cups of tea. I'm beginning to feel more like myself and anxious for answers.

My parents look worried and share many anxious looks and I say weakly, "Please tell me what happened?"

My mother takes hold of my hand and my father the other one. She says softly, "You were in a terrible car accident darling. I'm afraid you suffered a head injury and have been in a coma for several weeks."

I stare at her in confusion. "I know but it was Richard, not the car accident. He tried to kill me."

My mother looks so upset I regret my words. Shaking her head, she says, "I'm afraid Richard didn't survive the accident. He was propelled through the windscreen and died instantly."

I shake my head in confusion. "No, that's wrong. It was Ellie Matthews. We hit the girl on Gander Green lane. She hit the windscreen and died. Richard killed her and left me to take the blame."

The look they share worries me and I start to shake. My mother says quickly, "Take it easy darling. It's the shock. Don't speak about it anymore."

I shake my head wildly. "Richard killed her and then left. He told me I would pay. I'm to go to prison, officer Jones told me."

My father stands and punches a button to the left of the bed and I stare at it in disbelief. The panic button, why is it here? Is officer Jones being called to take me away? My mother reaches out and hugs me tightly. "I'm so sorry, Sarah. I wish things were different but all I care about is that you're safe and well."

Tony enters with my father and I look at him in surprise. "Tony, why are you my doctor? You're a police officer." My voice breaks. "You left me. You never came back."

He smiles kindly and sits beside me on the bed. "Sarah, you're confused. It's not uncommon for patients who have been in a coma to experience things in their subconscious. Everything that happened prior to the accident has mixed with events afterwards and created memories that are distorted."

I look at him in disbelief. "Are you saying I've been dreaming? All of this... the last few weeks. Everything I went through... was in my... head?"

He nods and I sink back against the pillows struggling to understand what they're telling me. "But the girl, Ellie Matthews, she's real... right?"

Tony shakes his head. "There was no girl, Sarah. It was just you and your husband. A witness saw you arguing as you turned into Gander Green lane. Another one saw your husband punch you in the face and your head hit the window. Then they saw him lose control of the car and the car hit a nearby tree at speed. Your husband wasn't wearing a seatbelt and was projected through the windscreen. A passer-by found you and pulled you from the car. There was nobody else there."

The tears fall freely as everything slots into place. We didn't kill the girl. She wasn't there. Richard died and the last few weeks have all been in my mind.

The next day my parents visit again and I can tell they have something on their mind. I recognise the awkward looks and say wearily, "What is it?"

My mum shakes her head and looks worried. "I'm sorry, Sarah. We didn't want to say anything yesterday because we thought it would all be too much to take in."

I feel worried and she smiles reassuringly. "I'm sorry darling but yesterday was Richard's funeral. They had to go and organise it because nobody knew if you would… I mean… ever come around."

She looks so worried and I shake my head. "Was Richard buried or cremated, mum?"

She shakes her head sadly. "Cremated darling."

My mind struggles to get a grip as I whisper, "What time?"

She looks surprised. "I'm not sure, I think it was around the same time you woke up."

I just stare into space as I remember back to yesterday – in my head, anyway. Richard was there all the time. He said so. He was always in my head since that fateful night. He never left me just like he said and it was only when he was set on fire, I was rid of him for good. That was what happened. Richard burned to set me free. It all makes sense. He controlled me to the very end. He tried to take me with him. He tried to drag me with him in death, hoping my heart would give out. Hoping I wouldn't pull through and he could chain me to him in the afterlife.

I whisper, "I was too strong for you, Richard. You never won; it was me."

Now I know why the house was in my name alone. I am the survivor. I was always going to be. Nothing he could do could change that fact and I will live where he has died. I have won.

I feel a lightness to my spirit that hasn't been there for some time as the reality sinks in. However, the looks on my parents faces tells me they haven't finished yet.

"My mum blinks away the tears as she says shakily, "I'm sorry darling but they couldn't save the baby."

I just stare at her in shock. The baby. What baby?

I think back to the crib rocking in the punishment room. The sounds of the newborn baby filling my head and I say shakily, "What baby?"

My mother s voice breaks as she says, "You were pregnant, darling. In the early stages but still a few weeks gone. I'm so sorry."

I turn my head to the side and blink away the tears. I was pregnant – with Richard's baby. The one thing he wanted above everything and the one thing that would chain me to his side forever. I lost our baby and I hate myself for feeling an overwhelming sense of relief that I did.

My parents say nothing and let me grieve but I feel like a fraud. How can I grieve for something I never wanted in the first place? Richard's baby would have been a constant reminder of him and a situation I had no control of. I know part of that baby was me but it was the weak part of me I hated. No, I can't grieve for something I never wanted. If it's anything, the emotion I'm feeling is relief.

Chapter Twenty-Six

Of all possessions a friend is the most precious.
Herodotus

Two days later Gloria visits me. As I see her anxious face come through the door I smile. She races over holding a huge bunch of yellow roses and says with emotion, "Thank God, Sarah. I've been so worried about you."

As she leans over to hug me, I smile and say warmly, "Thank you, Gloria."

She blushes a little and waves her hand, "For what?"

"For being here for me through this whole ordeal. The nurse told me you were my only visitor, well only welcome one, anyway."

Apparently, Sylvia did visit me that day. The doctors had to pull her away when she attacked me while I lay in my coma. I don't believe they pressed charges, but she was forbidden from contacting me again.

Gloria shakes her head. "They said you were only allowed one person to sit with you. I appointed myself even though the rest of the neighbours wanted to take a turn. You know, we've all been so worried about you. What happened was truly dreadful and when they told us Richard punched you, we were in total shock."

I shrug. "That doesn't matter."

She looks at me guiltily. "It does matter, Sarah because I saw the signs and chose to ignore them. I saw the light had died in your eyes a long time ago and never thought to question it. Angela told us you were at the council offices that day and now we know why you were really there. We let you down because none of us spotted the signs and if we did, we chose to ignore them."

I smile sadly. "Richard was clever. He started this lie a long time ago, and I never saw it coming. I'm guessing he fabricated a story of my mental stress over not being able to get pregnant and you put everything down to that."

She nods. "We were afraid to raise the subject because he told us it would do more harm than good. I feel so bad about it, which is probably why I wanted to be here for you now."

She reaches out and we clasp our hands together which means more to me than any words she can say.

I smile gratefully. "Thank you for the clothes and other things you brought. My mum told me you're the one who was responsible for the personal items and the pyjamas and dressing gown. You are so kind."

She shrugs. "As I said, I wanted to help. A little late but I got there in the end."

I'm not sure if I should say anything but I have to know.

"I'm sorry to ask this, Gloria, but what happened on the night of your 30th birthday?"

I see her cheeks blush and she looks uncomfortable. I smile reassuringly and she sighs. "I'm sorry but things got a little out of hand. When you left, we carried on the party and I blame it on the alcohol because I let them do things they shouldn't. When I woke the next morning, I was so ashamed."

She looks mortified and says quickly, "I promise you it only happened the once and signified the beginning of the end of my marriage."

I nod in agreement. "Same."

She looks shocked. "What, why?"

I shrug and says lightly, "Richard was never the same after that night. He told me I had let him down, and he spent the rest of our marriage punishing me for not being the perfect wife."

She shakes her head and says in a small voice, "I'm sorry."

Grasping her hand tightly, I say softly, "Why did it affect your marriage?"

She sighs heavily. "Because after that night, Edward saw me differently. Even though he was the one who set the whole thing up, he couldn't come to terms with what we did… what we all did. He hated the image of me with another man and we had terrible arguments. I suppose that's why I started something with Byron. My marriage was now a sham, and I craved a man's affection."

I have to know and say, "Did you ever… um… you know… with Richard after that night?"

She looks shocked. "No, I swear we never. It was only the once, and I felt so ashamed I couldn't look him in the eye for months. After a while, the memory faded but the recriminations just increased. If I was glad about one thing it was that you were never dragged into it. I never thought for one moment that he was doing what he did to you. None of us did. I thought you were the lucky one. You had escaped the madness, and I thought we had all learned a valuable lesson that night. Once again, it appears I was wrong."

For a while, we sit together and talk things through. We discuss everything that happened to us both and I discover that Gloria has suffered in her own way just as much as I did. If anything, it makes us stronger and cements our friendship for the future. I learn that she's divorcing Edward who has already moved in with another woman who he has been seeing for years. She doesn't seem upset by that and is just looking forward to the future – as am I.

Overall, I spend one more week in the hospital and on the day I leave, I walk between my parents to the car. They are driving me home to the place I feared for so long.

We turn into Gander Green lane and I stare at the pretty house that holds such a dear place in my heart. As we make to move past, I say loudly, "Stop."

My mother looks worried and I smile reassuringly. "Please. I just need a moment."

They leave me alone as I walk to the little picket fence. I stand beside it as I look out into the road that looks so peaceful now. Only good things happen in Gander Green lane, that hasn't changed. It delivered me my freedom which is why I will always be grateful to it.

As I stare at the spot where the accident happened, I'm aware that the little gate behind me opens. Spinning around, I see a man coming out looking at me curiously.

He smiles and says gently, "You're Sarah Standon, aren't you?"

I look at him in surprise and say, "Yes, how do you know?"

Offering me his hand, he says warmly, "I was there the night of the accident and was the first one on the scene and called the police. I'm so sorry for your loss."

As I take his hand, I remember the strong arms that pulled me away from the body I cradled in my arms. I remember those arms wrapping me in safety and promising that everything would be alright. The voice is familiar and brings comfort to my soul. His eyes are kind and his face gentle and strong. The tears once again form in my eyes as I whisper, "Thank you."

He looks embarrassed. "For what? I did what any other person with an ounce of compassion would do."

Just for a moment, I stare into those eyes and see something so precious it takes my breath away. He is different. Not all men are like Richard, I can see that now. Some men are kind, genuine and compassionate and I was just unlucky to find the opposite.

As I shake his hand, I say softly, "You know, I often used to see your wife when I drove by every day."

He looks confused. "I'm sorry, you must be mistaken. I live alone."

I stare at him in confusion and he smiles gently. "Maybe you've mistaken it for next door. A lady lives there, although she's much older than me."

I remain silent but I know what I saw. I can see my parents waiting and smile. "Anyway, thank you, Mr…?"

He smiles. "Matthews. Sam Matthews."

As I turn away, my heart settles. Of course, he is.

Epilogue
Twenty years later

"I'm off mum."

"Remember to take your coat. It's chilly out there and you'll catch your death if you go without one."

I hear her laughter echo through the rooms of the small cottage.

"You worry too much."

Rolling my eyes, I say firmly, "I mean it, do as I say for once in your life."

She shrugs on the huge padded coat and smiles. "I won't be long. One circuit of the park and then I'll be back."

Nodding, I say firmly, "Make sure that's all because we have a lot to do before the guests arrive."

As she heads towards the door, I smile. My daughter, the person I love unconditionally and the one I would do absolutely anything for to make her life her a happy one. Today is her 18th birthday and we have invited the whole family. My parents, her friends and Uncles and Aunts. Yes, there is a lot to prepare."

Sam comes in from the garden and slings a strong arm around my shoulders, kissing me gently on the cheek. "Hey, babe. I could murder a coffee."

I smile. "Sure. Have you sorted the gazebo out outside?"

He nods with amusement. "Yes."

"Have you mowed the lawn?"

"Yes."

"Have you watered the plants?"

"Yes, ma'am."

He grabs hold of me and as I wriggle in his arms, he kisses me deeply and I melt into him. My husband. The one I was always meant to marry.

"Yuk, for goodness sake I'm trying to eat breakfast here."

Laughing, we look over at Grady our son and I say teasingly, "What's the matter, don't you like seeing how much your parents love each other?"

He pretends to gag. "Disgusting. You're too old to have feelings."

Laughing, Sam ruffles his hair and pretends to get him in a headlock. Just for a minute, I watch them fooling around and smile to myself. I love this. I love them all – my family.

Nineteen years ago, I married Sam Matthews. We kept in touch and discovered a connection that neither of us could ignore. We married quickly and I moved into the house in Gander Green lane where we have lived ever since.

We have a happy life here and we used the money from 15 Richmond Avenue to pay off the mortgage and invest in rental properties nearby. Part of the money I received was donated to a shelter helping victims of domestic abuse and I volunteer there most days, helping women much like I was. My family mean everything to me and as I always thought, life in Gander Green lane is just perfect.

I spy the hat on the side and grabbing it, run to the front door. As I open it, I see my daughter heading through the picket gate with Bobby our little black terrier. As I see them my heart bursts with love for my perfect daughter who brings me so much joy. As Bobby barks at the cat across the road, her laughter floats across to me and I smile. Then I call, "Ellie, you forgot your hat."

She looks back and our eyes connect. She smiles as she did many years previously and I see the genuine love shining out from them as she says, "Thanks, mum. I promise I won't be long."

I throw her the hat and she catches it as it sails over the little picket fence. As she turns to jog down Gander Green lane everything is perfect as I always knew it would be.

The end